A PLACE IN MY HEART

A Place In My Heart

To Love Again Where Love Remains

DARCY WIEMERS

Melanie Fracchia

Darcy Wiemers

Contents

COPYRIGHT

First Published in 2022

.

ISBN 978-0-6453916-4-0 (Paperback Version)

ISBN 978-0-6453916-5-7 (E-book Version)

Cover Images: Canva Pro

Cover Design: Melanie Fracchia, Frac and Co Creative.

DEDICATION

In writing *A Place In My Heart* the storyline covers situations where some of the characters have their lives impacted by violent acts and speak out about their experiences under the guise of organisations which address such problems. I dedicate this book to two actual organisations I'm aware of who campaign to stop or prevent violence in Australian Society, which causes so much grief and pain to those effected

----

Danny Green's Coward Punch Campaign
Coward Punch Campaign – Stop The Coward Punch

The Luke Batty Foundation - to assist women and children affected by domestic violence – Founder Rosie Batty
Rosie Batty - Wikipedia
Rosie Batty Continues to Strive for Change - Australian Childhood Foundation

----

ALSO
To my wife Lorrain and daughter Melanie Fracchia, without whose assistance and support I would not be able to devote the time and effort to write this novel

ABOUT THE AUTHOR

I am the Author of two published novels (1) *Kimberley Kindred Spirits* - an Ebook Published with Amazon KDP and (2) *Love that goes Above & Beyond* - a Paperbook and Ebook published with Ingramspark. I have completed a Novel Writing Course and a Script Writing All Media Course with TAFE College, Brisbane, Queensland. I have an Associate Diploma in Aboriginal & Torres Strait Islander Cultural Studies, TAFE College, Cairns, Queensland. I am the author of tourism related articles for Travel Magazines as well as writing for various newsletters, plus short stories and articles for magazines and competitions. I worked for Queensland Tourism for over 25years travelling extensively throughout Australia and overseas, including travel to all the areas featured in this novel.

Chapter One

Sam Mackenzie's return to his hometown, Mt. Isa, was one which filled him with mixed emotions following his successful mission, with his mate Billy *Blue* Williams, to apprehend the murderer of his beautiful wife, Chloe, and their unborn son, Waru. The capture of Jimmy Johnson had afforded him immediate relief, knowing justice had been served for himself but more importantly for his family. Even though he believed he was coming to terms with his grief, he still felt a deep sense of loss and a daily battle to understand and accept what the future held for his life in the months and years ahead.

The capture of Chloe's killer was significant. Also, the exercise of communication that Sam was advised to undertake with the writing of love letters to Chloe, expressing his feelings. The most mystifying part of that was through the process of automatic writing, wherein he received, occasionally, a return message from his beloved Chloe and in what appeared to be her handwriting. He wasn't sure if it was Chloe actually communicating with him from the spirit world or if it was him expressing what he wanted to happen and somehow imitating her writing style.

His dilemma now was whether to acknowledge as truth the last message he received, wherein Chloe had given him permission to move on and find love again with someone else. The thought running through his head was, *'is it too early to even consider moving on to another relationship when I still have such lingering feelings for Chloe?'* This thought was prompted by the friendship he had developed with Letitia, a wonderful woman he'd met and spent time with frequently while searching for Chloe's killer and for whom he was now developing deep feelings.

Sam's mate Blue was someone whose opinion he valued, so visited him with the purpose of getting his advice on the practicality of pursuing not only a friendship with Letitia but determining if they could move beyond the friend's stage to a deeper relationship. Blue, together with his partner Aimee, who he'd met while staying in the Gemfields of Central Queensland, greeted Sam with an enthusiastic handshake from Blue while Aimee encircled him with a warm, welcoming hug.

'Look at you, Sam,' she commented. 'You're looking all relaxed and ready for action. What are you up to?'

'Oh, I just thought I'd catch up with my two favourite friends for a chat and see how you're going. Maybe have a debrief about what transpired while we were together down in the Gemfields, not to mention how you're both getting on. Anything happening in the way of engagement announcements, or is that *jumping the gun* as they say?'

'Well, strange you should ask, old mate,' prompted Blue. 'We've planned a party for the coming weekend and invited all our friends and family and we were just about to ring you to see if you were free and share with you some special news. Guess who's coming along?'

'I don't know, the Lord Mayor or some such dignitary, seeing you're such a well-known and popular local identity.' Sam was fairly sure he knew who it would be, but to be mysterious, he played along with their little charade.

'No, not a dignitary or a celebrity, but someone much more important,' Aimee excitedly proclaimed. 'Letitia is coming and is looking forward to catching up with us all again, but especially you. What do you think about that, Sam?'

'The sneaky thing. I was only on a mobile call to her a few nights ago and she didn't mention anything about visiting Mt. Isa, let alone attending your engagement party.'

'Well, that's partly our fault. We wanted to surprise you personally with the news of our engagement, and we were sure you wouldn't mind a visit from a special someone who seems to have created more than a little interest for you,' informed Aimee.

'That's certainly a pleasant surprise. However, the reason I wanted to talk to you both was to get some clarity in my mind about where my relationship with Letitia should go. Do we stay only friends, or should we pursue something deeper and more meaningful? On one hand, I still love my wife Chloe while I'm also developing deep feelings for Letitia, and I believe she does for me. Letitia also lost her future husband tragically and would still have feelings for him. So, we're sort of *stuck between a rock and a hard place* and not sure how to proceed. At least I am.'

'Yeah, that's something Blue and I discussed when we were planning to invite Letitia. You mentioned to us that recently, in the dialogue process you undertook, you believed Chloe gave you permission to move on. Meaning, therefore, you are free to pursue a deeper, more meaningful relationship with Letitia without feeling guilty. I agree with Chloe's sentiment that you deserve to be happy again. So Blue and I agreed you should let nature take its course. In your heart, do you think you're ready?'

'What I know, in my heart, is that we have a lot in common. We are both First Nations people, although from different tribal areas. This means we value the connection we have with our traditions, our culture, and the land where we were born. Whenever I was with her in the Gemfields, exploring the Carnarvon Gorge National Park or enjoying her company in Rockhampton, we had a great time. She's so easy to talk to and, as you know, gives great hugs. We've held hands just the once, but we haven't kissed yet. I guess when that happens, we'll know if there's a spark. I'm feeling nervous, like it's the first time when you're a teenager and you're with a girl you fancy.'

'I don't think you need our advice, Sam,' enthused Blue. 'I know your love for Chloe was one for the ages, but you've got to accept that you deserve to be in love and happy again. What you don't want to do is view Letitia through the same prism as Chloe. They are two entirely different people, with different ways of seeing the world. So don't expect everything to be like it was with Chloe. Keep an open mind and find the things that are special to you two. Just be yourself and we're sure everything will work out, just as it has for Aimee and I.'

'Thanks for your sage advice, Blue, and also your opinion, Aimee, from a woman's point of view. I love you both and appreciate you have my and Letitia's best interests in mind. I can't wait now for the weekend and to explore the deeper connection that's developing with Letitia.'

Chapter Two

When Sam Mackenzie entered the Mt. Isa Civic Centre Auditorium, it amazed him to see the place packed with invitees eager to celebrate with Billy *Blue* Williams and his fiancée Aimee, their engagement. Sam knew Blue was a well-known figure in the area because he had built a reputation from his sporting achievements and representing the interests of the local community. The esteem and affection in which the locals held him was clear from comments Sam overheard as he moved from group to group, making contact once more with people he had not seen since he had left his home to pursue his career with the Queensland Police Service in Brisbane.

Eventually, Sam caught up with Blue and Aimee when they could free themselves from the hugs and kisses of some close friends. 'Hey you two, congratulations. How lucky were we to decide to travel to the Gemfields of Central Queensland to become prospectors, Blue? Otherwise, you wouldn't have been lucky enough to have met such a beautiful and compatible partner, in Aimee.'

'I told you it was my sense of humour that did it. Girls like blokes who make them laugh. It helps them feel safe,' replied Blue. 'Anyhow, you weren't exactly a shrinking violet in using your charms to attract a beautiful woman. What about you and the lovely Letitia?'

'How true, Blue. Having just mentioned her, I'm wondering where she is. I thought she'd be here by now,' replied Sam.

Those words had hardly left his lips when from behind he was embraced in a firm hug and greeted by a hearty laugh that he knew could only come from the mischievous woman they were just talking about.

Sam instantly turned to take full advantage of the best hugger he knew and to return with strength and warmth the feelings he experienced from contact with Letitia. He brushed a gentle kiss on her cheek, which Letitia returned with a full-on kiss on Sam's lips. He felt practically breathless and voiceless for several seconds with this new surprise greeting, not sure how to respond. Gaining his composure, he blurted out his response to Letitia's public show of affection. 'Wow, you sure know how to announce your arrival. Mind you, I'm not complaining,' Sam commented with an encouraging smile.

As Blue and Aimee faded into the crowd, enjoying what they had just witnessed and basking in the joy of seeing their plan coming to fruition. They were aware from their time spent in the Gemfields with Sam and Letitia that the journey back from the pain and grief of both losing their loved ones in tragic circumstances could only be helped by accepting the past and moving on. They'd decided their mission was to facilitate the process of Sam and Letitia realising they could find the path to happiness again by reaching out to each other for comfort, compassion and hopefully love.

'You're truly a welcome sight Sam, I've missed your smiley face and your genuine caring nature in helping me to come to terms with the loss of my fiancée, Mike. The process you showed me of writing love letters to him was a freeing experience. I hope you didn't think I was too forward in kissing you, but I've genuinely missed you and seeing you again it overwhelmed me with so much joy my response just happened, spontaneously.'

'Please don't apologise, Letitia. We've hugged and held hands previously and I have wanted to kiss you but wasn't sure how or when that would happen, considering what we have both experienced. It's hard moving on from those we've loved, knowing in our hearts they are still a part of each of us, but I'm sure they would want us to find happiness again. I think it is with love and respect for those we've lost that will enable us to move on.'

'Okay, let's have some fun,' enthused Letitia. 'There's a live band over there. Let's join the newly engaged couple and *shake a leg* in the tradition of our indigenous heritage.'

As the night developed, Sam and Letitia danced and genuinely enjoyed being with their best friends, Blue and Aimee, who took them around the guests, introducing them to all the people who were significant in their lives. These included Blue's family and Aimee's mum and dad, who had travelled up from Longreach to celebrate their daughter's engagement.

The celebrations were winding down as the clock approached midnight, with the band bursting into the music for *Show Me The Way To Go Home.* Presently they changed to the famous *Men at Work* song, *Do you come from a Land Downunder* with all the guests forming into a Conga line around the perimeter of the room and joining in with the chorus, *Do you come from a Land Downunder, where women glow and men plunder? Can't you hear, can't you hear the thunder? You better run; you better take cover.* This continued to the front door where Blue and Aimee were standing to thank everyone for coming and sharing in one of the most significant times in their lives.

Bidding their fond farewell to their happily engaged friends, Sam and Letitia made their way to Letitia's hotel where on arrival she asked Sam if he would like to come to her room for coffee and catch up on all that had been happening since they were last together in the Carnarvon Gorge National Park, where Letitia was a Park Ranger.

When they'd settled into a comfortable outdoor lounge on the balcony, their conversation turned to how each of them was coping with their feelings. Writing love letters to their departed loved ones was their process of addressing their grief. They both agreed they were moving forward with a more positive outlook, especially as their friendship was now developing into something more meaningful.

Turning to face Letitia and look directly into her eyes, Sam reached out to take her hands in his. 'You know Letitia, before our chance meeting in Rubyvale, I was really struggling emotionally because having your partner torn from your life so dramatically as Chloe had been takes you to some dark places, as I'm sure also experienced. The furthest thing from my mind was finding someone else to love, as I couldn't conceive there was ever going to be someone to replace Chloe and the love I felt for her. The stage we are now reaching makes me think that not only is a relationship with you possible, but I'm hoping deep down it is inevitable. What are your feelings or thoughts?'

'Sometimes, Sam, I think it best not to question fate or kismet. I believe in letting life take its natural course. The night I walked into that restaurant, I didn't know Aimee was even going to be there. I went there on the off chance I'd bump into someone I knew to have a drink with. Since Michael died from that senseless *one coward punch,* I had been drifting along with a feeling of hopelessness. I just trust and believe that good things happen if you open yourself up to the possibility there are events in life that are beyond our control. So, what I say is, no matter how our meeting came about, let's embrace it and hope we both find what we are looking for. In my case, to love again and to be loved in return. I know it's hard moving on from someone you've loved and lost, but loneliness and heartbreak create a toll that only love can remedy. If I'm interpreting it right, I think we're both looking for the same thing.'

'Thanks for putting into words similar sentiments to my own. I think now we have established this solid foundation of understanding it is something we can build upon and not feel guilty we are betraying the genuine feelings we had for our departed partners. They will always be a part of our lives, for love is something that is universal, encompassing all kinds of relationships.' With those comments, their faces moved voluntarily to meet in a passionate kiss and an empowering embrace.

'What a beautiful way to end a fantastic evening and to start a new and beautiful journey towards a new life of hope and happiness. Before I go can I ask what you are doing tomorrow, Letitia?'

'We've been so busy having fun and enjoying each other's company I haven't had the chance to talk to you about what else Blue has planned for me while I'm here. You remember the *Stop the coward punch* campaign I got involved with in Rockhampton with Michael's mother, well Blue thought it would be a great opportunity to address the local Mt. Isa sporting clubs and community to spread the message of the senselessness of such stupidity. From my experience, I can relate to how much it affects so many people. I believe personal testimony is powerful. I was wondering if you would like to come along to support me as I'm extremely nervous, having not been involved in much public speaking.'

'That sounds great, Letitia. I'm so proud of you for spreading the message of something that is still fresh and deeply painful. I'd be happy to be up on stage with you for support and you can also call on me to talk about how losing someone through an act of violence creates such grief. Where and when is it taking place?'

'Thanks for that, Sam. I'm immediately relieved. I was shaking in my shoes, wondering how I'd cope, but with you there, I'll be so much at ease. All the sporting clubs are gathering at Buchanan Park Events Complex at 1.00pm. So, if you arrive here about 11.30am we can have a quick lunch and make our way there. Come here, you beautiful man.' With those words, a lingering kiss and affirming hug, they reluctantly parted with feelings and emotions coursing through their bodies for the prospects of what wonderful, unimaginable moments of joy lay before them.

Chapter Three

When Sam and Letitia, along with the organiser of the event, Billy *Blue* Williams and his fiancé Aimee arrived at the Buchanan Park Events Complex, it surprised them that the main Kalkadoon Arena held such a large representation of local sporting and community organisations. Obviously, the *Stop the Coward Punch* campaign was one which resonated with large sections of the local Mt. Isa population.

Onto the stage set up in the centre of the arena, the group made their way to the podium, accompanied by the welcome sound of clapping. As it slowly receded, Blue stepped up to the microphone. 'I'd first like to pay respects to the Kalkadoon First Nations People, on whose land we are gathered, and to all Traditional Owners, their Elders, past, present and emerging.'

'Thanks everyone for coming and for your welcome,' he continued. 'We are here today to address the growing concern of the *one punch kills* problem. Some of you will probably have experienced the effects on a person you know or someone you've heard of whose lives have been ravaged because of senseless, needless violence that is avoidable. Some of you may have even lost a loved one. The statistics speak for themselves. Eighty-two percent of victims experience lost consciousness or severe brain impact. The worst-case scenario is that many never regain consciousness. We have two special guests here today who have both experienced the loss of a loved one through the result of senseless violent acts. My first guest speaker is Letitia Morris. She is a proud Karingbal First Nations person, who works as an Indigenous Park Ranger in the Carnarvon Gorge National Park. The next speaker, who many of you already may know because he grew up here, is Detective Sergeant Sam Mackenzie, a proud Kalkadoon First Nations person, currently on bereavement leave from the Queensland Police, Brisbane. So first, please welcome Letitia.'

'Hi everyone, thanks for turning out to listen to this important message. I lost my partner, Michael, to a *cowardly one punch attack* just months before we were to be married. He was out with his football mates at a local hotel celebrating their Rugby League Grand Final victory. I don't know if it was an irate fan from the opposition team or just some macho maniac out to show how tough he was. Without notice or provocation, this bloody idiot, excuse the language, king hit him from behind, knocking Michael to the concrete floor. That one punch plus contact with the hard surface knocked him unconscious. He couldn't be revived, and his parents had the soul-destroying decision of having to turn off his life support. Until you see the effects on the parents having to agree to turn off the life support of their child, then you can't appreciate how much they suffer. Much worse is the reality they will never recover. For myself, I also suffer from the aftermath of Michael's death and am still trying to come to terms with the grief. It is not only the physical loss but coming to terms with the hopes and dreams we had for each other that will be no more. Thanks to my good friends Blue and his partner Aimee and to this wonderful man beside me, Sam Mackenzie, I am seeing the light of day after being in a dark place. I feel life is still worth living, but will always feel the loss of a loved one. Sam and I have been supporting each other through the loss of our loved ones. For his own story, please welcome Sam.'

Sam surveyed the faces of the people fixated on him as he picked up the microphone to speak. 'I first met Letitia when Blue and I were pretending to be prospectors looking for gems and opals at Anakie and Rubyvale in central Queensland. When I say pretending, I mean we used that as an excuse to find out if the mongrel, excuse the language, who murdered my beautiful wife, Chloe, was hiding out in the region where he had relatives. This wasn't a case of the one punch scenario referred to by Letitia, but it was just as devastating from the aspect of how violence destroys lives. Chloe was a fellow Police officer who was gunned down attending a domestic violence incident. I can't find the words to describe the grief I felt but also Chloe's parents experienced and will never recover from. Not only did they lose their daughter and me, my wife, but Chloe was pregnant with their grandson and our son. Similar to Letitia, I am also dealing with the grief from loss, and we are helping each other. The point I want to reinforce is the grief that is caused to so many people because of senseless, needless violence that is avoidable.' Sam paused to check if his message was connecting with the crowd and, satisfied it was, he continued.

'Concentrating today on the *coward punch campaign,* this is something you can all be conscious of and think about before you act out of anger or of a need to impose yourself physically on someone else for whatever reason. I assure there is never a valid reason. As a police officer, I have seen firsthand victims of the so-called *one punch attack* and to advise you, there are no winners. The victim and their families and friends suffer the most, but the perpetrator and his family don't escape. A jail sentence negatively changes the lives of the perpetrator and their families. So, I am here to reinforce the message Letitia has so strongly imparted. *Think before you act.* Thanks for listening and please heed the words of someone who has suffered and will for the rest of my life.'

Blue stepped up to the microphone to advise everyone present that representatives of the organisations gathered at the meeting had agreed to form a working committee to continue to spread the message throughout the area, including local schools and entertainment venues. 'Thanks for such a terrific turnout. I am pleased I've been able to instigate this meeting and apologise that I can't be on the committee as I have recently become engaged to my beautiful Aimee and am moving away. Her folks have asked us to help them run their cattle property outside Longreach, so that's where we are heading next. Goodbye and, as we often hear, *be kind to each other.*'

******

The four friends gathered that evening at the hotel where Letitia stayed to celebrate the last meal they thought they'd have together for some time.

'Well, Aimee and I know what we're doing in the future, although I've got to learn quickly how to look after cattle and all the things relating to operating a large cattle station,' said Blue. 'What about you two?'

'I'm just cooling my heels here in Mt. Isa until I get called up to give evidence in the court case in Brisbane for Jimmy Johnston. That should be soon. There are also court cases pending for Curly Jacobs and Charlie Briggs into the cattle rustling and drug running, not to mention my assault and kidnapping, so I think things might get busy in the next couple of months.'

'That only leaves you, Letitia. Have you got to be back at work as a Ranger soon?' questioned Aimee.

'I've taken a week off to come up to see you guys, but I have extra leave due that I can take. It's coming into our quiet season at Carnarvon Gorge as far as visitors are concerned, so I can take extra time if you have something planned. I've just got to let them know.'

'Blue and I are ready to head to Longreach and I thought if you both had nothing urgent pending, you might like to accompany us and help us settle into our new surroundings. Are you both up for that?'

'Let me get back to you tomorrow, Aimee, after I let them know at the Visitor Centre in Carnarvon Gorge,' advised Letitia.

'I should be free until I hear from my police contacts about when court cases are happening. So, I'll see you and Blue tomorrow, Aimee,' replied Sam.

Upon Blue and Aimee's departure, Letitia took Sam into her arms in an affectionate embrace as she kissed him, lingering longer than previously. 'I don't know how I could have gotten through my talk today if you hadn't been there. You give me so much strength, support, and comfort. Any time being with you just helps me to feel stronger and I look forward to us spending some extra days together helping Aimee and Blue settle in. See you tomorrow. Sweet dreams Sam.'

When Sam arrived at his car, there was an envelope lodged under the windscreen wipers. The interior light of his vehicle was enough for him to read the contents of a brief letter, roughly scribbled on the back of the flyer used to invite people to the meeting they had spoken at earlier. It didn't beat about the bush as to its message.

I'm glad I went to the rally today and saw you and your lovely girlfriend. You're the mongrel copper who arrested one of our brothers many years ago in Brisbane. You ruined his life. After he went to jail, his wife left him taking his kids. He lost his house, car and everything he valued. He has vowed to make you pay now he's out of prison. I'm sure he'll be pleased to hear from me. A fortunate coincidence I was in Mt. Isa on another matter: Time for revenge copper. You won't know where or when. Be assured we're coming for you or your loved ones.

Chapter Four

Sam reluctantly accepted, as had most of his colleagues in the Criminal Investigation Branch, that the job came with threats from criminals who felt themselves unjustly treated or who had gripes like those expressed in the note left on his car. It wasn't something though that he took lightly, knowing the level of violence he had already experienced with the murder of his beloved Chloe. Sam took the precaution of advising the commander of Mt. Isa police district of the details of the threat so it would alert them to any incidents that could occur which may involve people with whom he had a relationship. As he had learnt in his police training, until someone made good on their threats, there is not a lot that could be done, especially in this circumstance which was anonymous.

Sam picked up Letitia from her hotel and, as had become their usual practice, greeted each other with an affectionate embrace that was more recently accompanied by a deep, lingering and passionate kiss. This was no exception as he parted with a smile that could light up the room. 'I think that starting my day like this can become a beautiful habit I am going to find hard to break,' a delighted Sam enthused.

'I'm hoping it becomes a habit, Sam, that doesn't have to end. I know we still have hurdles to cross over, but let's take each one at a time and see where we end up,' Letitia wisely advised.

Before going to their meeting with Blue and Aimee to discuss whether they would accompany the newly engaged couple on the move to Aimee's parents' cattle station outside Longreach, Sam explained to Letitia the letter he found attached to his vehicle.

'So, are you worried, Sam, or do you think it may be some whacko out to scare the hell out of you?'

'It's not something I'm prepared to ignore, nor is it a cause for alarm. If I'd put my life on hold because of the threats I've received as a police officer, I wouldn't be doing my job, let alone enjoying my life. We'll be cautious and careful. Besides, I'm here to keep you safe, Letitia.'

'Yes, my beautiful knight in shining armour,' assured Letitia, wrapping her arms around him and reinforcing it with a gentle kiss.

******

Sam and Letitia found Blue and Aimee packing up their belongings, ready for their move to the cattle station near Longreach. 'So, do we have two willing travellers to join us on our adventure into the world of cattle farming?' inquired Blue.

'I've contacted my office at Carnarvon Gorge, and I've got approval to take another week's leave. So, yeah. I'm willing, but I'm not too sure how helpful I'll be.

However, I have been out with my brother Mitchell when he's been rounding up cattle to take to the auctions, so I got a few clues from him that might come in handy,' shared Letitia.

'I'm keen to join you, Blue, but I need to alert you to something that happened after I left you last night.' Sam explained how he found a threatening anonymous letter when he went to his car and needed them to know before they accepted him as a travelling companion that the threats might be real. He didn't want them to feel unsafe or threatened.

'Bloody hell. No matter where you go these days, there's always someone trying to make life difficult for you. You know we've stuck together through thick and thin Sam, so don't give it another thought. Besides, you'll be safer out in the open plains of a cattle property than in Mt. Isa. Aimee and I will be ready in an hours' time, so if that suits, we'll meet back here and head off.'

They were soon on the road in two separate vehicles for the approximately seven-hour journey to Longreach and then thirty kilometres to the property of Aimee's parents. It was just past sundown as they approached a brightly lit, typical Australian country style building with bull-nosed, corrugated iron roofing protruding out over the surrounding verandas encircling the entire building. Their arrival was undoubtedly expected because a party atmosphere prevailed with people gathered around an outdoor barbeque area festooned with a variety of multi-coloured lights and festive balloons.

Aimee's parents greeted the arrivals, supported by an enthusiastic cheer of welcome from the gathered invitees. Blue, Aimee, Sam and Letitia were soon engulfed in the orderly greetings involving friendly backslapping, handshaking, hugs and kisses. As they moved around the group of well-wishers, Aimee introduced her travel companions to her other family and friends from surrounding properties, and business associates from Longreach who'd had a long relationship with the landowners.

'This is so overwhelming,' advised Aimee, addressing the friendly gathering. 'I never expected this. So many familiar faces. As you know, Blue, my fiancé and I are moving back home permanently and it's great for him to get to meet so many of you who are so important to us, all in one place. Thank you for that. I'm really so touched; I think I'm going to cry.' Aimee lost her composure and the tears of joy flowed.

Blue jumped into the breach to express his feelings. 'I have often heard of country hospitality, but this is truly above and beyond anything I could ever imagine. I feel so welcome, like I've already been around for some time. You might have to put up with my need to get up to speed quickly regarding helping to run a large cattle property, and I feel I can come to any of you for advice as we settle into this challenge. Our two dearest friends, Sam and Letitia, unfortunately, are only with us for a short time before they move on to the Carnarvon Gorge, so thanks for also welcoming them.'

Immediately, Blue had finished talking, a local country music band started playing, prompting the guests to sing along or break into some boot-scooting on a timber dance floor set up for the occasion. Music, dancing, eating, and drinking continued well into the evening before festivities wound up and the visitors departed.

'Let's leave this mess until tomorrow and get you guys settled in. You've had a long day and no doubt will welcome a comfortable bed,' indicated Aimee's dad. 'Aimee will show where to bunk down. I'll see you all in the morning and we'll take you on a tour around the property.'

Chapter Five

It had been a wonderfully educational and enjoyable time travelling around Aimee's family property, learning about the working life of an outback cattle station covering tens of thousands of hectares. When Sam and Letitia were ready to leave, having spent the week enjoying the laid-back lifestyle, they had confidence that Blue and Aimee would make a good fist at helping to run a cattle station.

'Thanks for allowing us to share this time with you, Blue and Aimee,' remarked Letitia as she and Sam were packed and ready to head towards Carnarvon Gorge. 'I guess next time we'll see you is at your wedding, hopefully soon. I'm so blessed to have bumped into you guys in the Rubyvale Hotel all those months ago. I don't know where I'd be today if I hadn't met you two, but especially my saviour Sam. It's hard to express the depth of despair and loneliness one feels with the loss of someone you love. Thanks for everything you've done to help me see I can find happiness again.' As Aimee, Blue, Letitia and Sam embraced in a group hug, tears of joy flowed freely and not just on the faces of the women.

The travel time to Carnarvon varied depending on which direction they headed. They'd only gone a short distance when Sam had the lingering feeling they should go via the Gemfields and call in on their mining companion, *old Bob*, to see how he had recovered from the trauma he'd experienced because of his discovery of drugs being grown on the Johnson property which led to the capture of Chloe's killer, Jimmy Johnson. Letitia agreed, and some four hours later, they pulled up to Bob's mining shack to be met with the enthusiastic barking and tail wagging of Bailey, Bob's blue heeler dog and best mate. They knocked on the door and could hear heavy breathing and a weak voice asking for help. Sam rushed to Bob's bed.

'Good God, old mate, you look in a bad way. What happened to you?' Bob struggled to talk but pointed to his chest. 'You may have an issue with your heart. We better get you to the ambulance in Rubyvale.' After making Bob as comfortable as possible in the van section at the back of the Four-Wheel drive, with Bailey keeping a cautious watch on his companion, they sped off, hoping they were not too late.

The ambulance in Rubyvale quickly assessed Bob and informed Sam and Letitia that it was lucky they found him when they did. 'We have to get him to the hospital in Emerald immediately. If he needs more treatment than they can provide, they'll fly him to Rockhampton. Give us your phone number and we'll let you know the outcome.'

Sam and Letitia were farewelling Bob while Bailey showed signs of distress for his sick mate. Bob requested in a weak voice if they would take care of Bailey. 'It's okay mate. You go with Sam and his friend. I'll see you soon.' Bailey gave a mournful cry as the paramedic closed the back door of the ambulance. Letitia could see he was so sensitive to the condition of Bob as she took Bailey into her arms to console him and shower him with the kindness she had experienced when her fiancé tragically died from a cowardly punch. She nursed the dog in its distress for the entire four-hour journey to Carnarvon Gorge. Along the way, she phoned her brother Mitchell and he and their father Ethan were waiting to welcome back Letitia, Sam and Bailey.

'Greetings, so great to see you both again. Looks like you picked up a passenger. Hello little fella,' said Ethan, as he reached out to pat Bailey. 'What's the story? He looks like he needs a good feed and he also looks kind of sad.'

Letitia explained what had transpired with *old Bob* and how Bailey was his constant companion. It was clear he needed some love until he could reunite with his best mate again.

'I've got the best remedy for him. We've got a friendly female cattle dog named Riley who Bailey can mix in with,' advised Mitchell. 'She'll mother him for sure. We'll feed him some good tucker as well.'

'Great Mitch. Glad to see you looking so good. You did some great work setting up those cattle rustlers for the police to nab red-handed in the act,' commented Letitia as they all settled down to enjoy a much-needed beer after a long and eventful day.

******

Letitia reported for work the next day at the Carnarvon Ranger Station, leaving Sam on his own to relax and soak in the environment's beauty with its myriad of natural flora and fauna. There were a variety of natural aromas wafting from surrounding foliage on the breeze, which Sam was enjoying. It lulled his senses as he drifted into a peaceful sleep state. Suddenly, he was jolted into consciousness by the shrill messaging of his phone. He grabbed it with alarm, not expecting contact from friends or family. He was more alarmed when he opened the message, threatening in its content.

Hi Copper. I guess you got the message left on your car in Mt. Isa. Bet you thought we couldn't track you down. Thanks to your mate Blue, he was very helpful in providing your movements when he introduced you and your lovely girlfriend during the recent 'coward punch rally'. It was easy to get your phone number when you have shady criminals as your friends. I knew you were heading to Longreach with Blue, which he outlined at the rally, and I deduced you would head to Carnarvon next. Guess what? I beat you here. Stay alert, Sam, especially for your lovely lady. She won't know when I'll strike!

Sam's immediate reaction was to contact Letitia on her mobile phone, but he felt he couldn't sit idly by knowing she could already be in danger. He had to find her quickly to allay his fears of how this unknown threat might play out. He drove at breakneck speed to the Ranger Station to find out if Letitia was escorting visitors on a tour around the Gorge. After finding out her location, Sam took off in an all-terrain vehicle to catch up with the group at one of the popular sites featuring cave paintings and carvings by Indigenous tribal members dating back thousands of years. He was relieved when he saw Letitia explaining to the visitors the significance of the artwork. On seeing Sam, she quickly excused herself to find out the reason for his appearance.

'Hi Sam, are you okay? You look stressed. What's the matter?'

'I got this text message,' explained Sam, handing her his phone. 'I had to get to you straight away to make sure nothing had happened to you.' Without thinking of what the tourists nearby might think, Sam wrapped his arms around Letitia in a protective embrace after she read the text message and emitted an audible gasp of horror.

'Oh my God, this is awful. What can we do?'

'Let's just try to keep calm. I'll stay here with you to complete the tour as normal. Just pretend as best you can that everything is okay. When we get back to the Ranger Station, we can figure out what to do.'

The tour soon completed satisfactorily to the vocal acclimation and compliments of the visitors, and Letitia was relieved to at last be in the safety of the Ranger Station. 'So, what happens next?' she asked.

'We don't really know if the person making these latest threats is actually here in the National Park or if he sent it from Mt. Isa and he is just trying to scare us. I was a bit puzzled when the message said, *"bet you thought we couldn't track you down."* I don't know what he meant by "*we*". Do we need to be on the lookout for more than one person? As a precaution, I intend to stay with you constantly. I hope you're comfortable with that?'

'To be quite honest, I'd be a dithering mess trying to do my daily duties if you weren't nearby, Sam. You make me feel so protected. Come here, my big, handsome bodyguard,' whispered Letitia into his ear as they melted into each other's arms, remaining passionately connected in their bond of security, realising the dependence they produced in each other.

Chapter Six

Sam, true to his promise of being Letitia's constant companion, never let her out of his sight or at least maintained awareness of where she was during the entire day. At the completion of her second guided tour of the Carnarvon Gorge cultural visitation sites, Letitia breathed a sigh of relief and a release of the tension which had built up from trying to observe every visitor, wondering if one of them had any intention of harming her. After the last of her group departed, she abandoned any pretence of being composed and sunk unashamedly into Sam's protective embrace. 'Thank God that day is over and we had no drama,' were the first words Letitia uttered with relief.

'Hopefully it will stay that way and the anonymous threats were only meant to scare us,' reinforced Sam. 'We'll check in at the Ranger Station on our way back to your cabin, so they know you are safe.'

It was usual practice for Rangers to check into the Station to debrief and discuss any concerns or issues which may have arisen during their tours. All had reported back except Ranger Stacey Roberts, who had taken a group to visit Cathedral Cave, featuring a panorama of rock imagery. It was one of the longer tours, but she should have returned by now, as her group had reported back and already departed the park. Attempts to reach her phone proved futile, so the officials in charge immediately put into place a search mission involving the Rangers who had returned. Sam volunteered after explaining that he was a member of the Queensland Police, currently on leave. He also felt it expedient to let staff know he had recently received a threat which he thought was only relevant to himself and Letitia and was the reason he accompanied her during her tours. As he awaited feedback in relation to what he had just explained, his phone dinged with a message.

Sorry to ruin your day, copper, but your macho act of protecting your girlfriend all day meant I've had to change my plans. I charmed the lovely Stacey and now she's safely in my care, if you could call it that. She's safe, for now, hidden away until I can make other arrangements. I'll be in touch.

There were audible expressions of concern and panic among all the staff and Rangers on receiving the details of Sam's message.

Sam knew he had to take charge as he was the person most experienced in situations where someone had been abducted and threats made about their safety. 'Let's not panic. First thing I need to do is phone Police contacts I know in Emerald. This is a kidnapping case, and it's wise not to waste time. They can be here in about three hours. In the meantime, we can start a search ourselves of areas close to where Stacey was conducting her tour. We have a couple of hours of light, so let's not delay. One other thing. Please don't go off on your own. Make sure there are always at least three of you together.'

'Before you go,' interrupted Letitia. 'While Sam was talking, I phoned my father, Ethan. He is a custodian of Carnarvon Gorge and some of the surrounding areas which relate to him being an elder of the Karingbal First Nations people, who are some of the traditional owners of the country on which we are standing. He has a thorough knowledge of the terrain and probable hiding places where Stacey's abductor could be holding her. My dad is an expert tracker, as is my brother Mitchell, who is also coming. They'll be here by the time we return.'

With their *all-terrain vehicles,* they sped as fast as the countryside, with its undulating curves and slopes, would allow. Each group was directed to a particular area, which included a possible hiding place, such as a cave. They searched without success until it became too dark to continue. By the time they'd returned to the Ranger Station, Letitia's father Ethan and brother Mitchell were waiting. Sam had also received a message from his police officer friend, Senior Constable Russell Hoffman, that he and a team were about an hour away. The person in charge of the Ranger Station operations, Indigenous leader Boolimba Moss, advised he had full confidence in Letitia's father taking charge and asked for his advice.

'There's not much we can do tonight, especially as you have already searched the most likely places Ranger Stacey may be held captive. Place a notice at the entrance to the park that all tours are cancelled until further advised. All you Rangers need to be careful returning home and to stay there until you hear from the chief Ranger. This is for your own safety and to allow ourselves and the police to do our jobs without extra distractions. So, goodnight and stay safe,' advised Ethan.

Ethan had just finished his address when Russell Hoffman pulled up to the Rangers' station with several vehicles in a convoy containing two police officers in each. Sam and Ethan quickly advised them about what had transpired and the plans for searching the Gorge and surrounding areas for any signs of Ranger Stacey and her captor. Boolimba Moss arranged for Russell and his fellow police officers to occupy a facility attached to the Station which contained enough beds and a kitchen so they would be comfortable during their stay.

'Looks like we're all settled then,' concluded Sam as he and Letitia, accompanied by her father and brother, made their way back to Letitia's cabin for the night. When they arrived there and Ethan and Mitchell alighted from their vehicle, there was a flurry of excitement as two dogs charged towards Sam and Letitia, each having an animal leaping up for their attention.

'Great to see you, Bailey. You can help us track down Ranger Stacey, seeing you did such a great job of finding your mate Bob when he'd been kidnapped and abandoned down a disused mineshaft. This must be Ethan and Mitchell's dog Riley,' expressed Sam, reaching out to show his affection for the animal, which had clearly connected with Bailey.

'Yes, they've become great mates and Bailey has responded with a new lease on life,' confirmed Ethan. 'Riley also has had her moments in finding people who have wandered off in the Gorge and become lost. I'm sure they'll be a big help tomorrow with our search.'

After spending a couple of hours discussing plans, eating dinner, and relaxing with a few beers, they all bunked down, ready for what the next day held in store for them.

Chapter Seven

Sam, Letitia, Ethan and Mitchell all arrived at the Carnarvon Ranger Station at 7.00am to find Boolimba Moss, a group of his Rangers and the police officers gathered around a conference table discussing the plan that would enable the maximum coverage to ensure they overlooked nothing in their search for Ranger Stacey Roberts. Boolimba proceeded to outline what he considered would be the most efficient way of covering the area where he believed Stacey might be held captive.

'I have checked out the photos and video surveillance that were transmitted from the site of Cathedral Cave, from where Stacey disappeared. After her visitors had departed, she was checking the area for any rubbish. The footage shows a man accosting her and appearing to inject her with something, causing her to collapse. He physically carries her and they disappear toward the location of Big Bend. We'll search Cathedral Cave first, then head towards Big Bend. We have eight all-terrain vehicles (ATV's), including the two that Officer Russell Hoffman brought and two belonging to Ethan and Mitchell. What I propose is that in each vehicle there is a police officer and a Ranger. Ethan and Mitchell will travel in front with Sam and Letitia and their two dogs. In each vehicle will be a two-way Walkie Talkie that will allow you to talk to each other instantly. I will remain here to monitor the operation and check on any live feed from other cameras strategically placed around the Gorge. Do you have anything to add, Russell?'

'We have a police dog trained to locate missing people, and with Ethan's two dogs, we should be able to cover a lot of territory. Two of our police officers are trained to operate Drones which have heat seeking capability to locate someone travelling undercover through dense forest country. So, we'll investigate around Cathedral Cave and then if we find nothing there, we'll journey towards Big Bend. If Stacey and her abductor are still in the Gorge, we should have a good chance of locating them. Anyone else have anything more that may assist our search?'

'Just one thing,' added Sam. 'The person who I suspect has abducted Stacey is the same one who has threatened me and appears to be associated with a man I imprisoned many years ago and blames me for how his life turned out. This person may be dangerous, so don't take any risks. The police officers are armed and should be the only ones to approach the perpetrator of this crime if you locate him.'

The convoy of ATV's sped off towards Cathedral Cave and on arrival began a thorough search of the surrounding area. It was difficult to tell much from a study of footprints as the tour group for that day moved extensively about the area. The dogs encircled the nearby surrounds but showed no sign of anything needing further checking. Considering the camera feed showed Stacey being taken towards Big Band, they headed to that destination. They drove at a slow pace in order to observe any telltale signs of departures from the main track. They'd been travelling some fifteen minutes when Ethan in the lead ATV pulled up abruptly, hopping out to study the area in front of him.

'See here,' he indicated, using his tracking experience gleaned from his Indigenous background and inherited knowledge. 'There's evidence that a vehicle pulled up here from the skid marks on the loose gravel caused by braking quickly. There are footprints leading from his all-terrain vehicle, heading into the bush, then again coming back to the vehicle. Note, however, that the outward footprints are deeper than those on the return, suggesting if this is Ranger Stacey's abductor, he may have carried her out but returned on his own. The footprints disappear when he traverses rocky ground. I can see about half a kilometre away a wall of sandstone running east-west for some distance, where it's possible there could be some caves. An ideal place to hide someone. Russell, if you and five of your police officers go east with your trained dog, I'll head off with the rest of the group towards the west with our dogs, Bailey and Riley.' Ethan produced one of Stacey's garments for the dogs to get a good sniff of and took off.

Bailey was excited, leaping about and pulling on his leash. Upon his release, he shot off at express pace, sniffing as he ran, followed by Riley and further back Ethan's group. It was mostly uphill, so they laboured in the heat trying to keep up. They weren't sure where Bailey had disappeared to until, some distance away, they could hear his frantic barking that was quickly accompanied by those of Riley. As they came into sight of the dogs at the entrance of a cave, it was clear by their leaping about they had found, hopefully, what they were looking for. Ethan was the first to enter, producing a torch attached to his belt to search the gloomy interior. He heard a weak moan and rushed deeper to discover Ranger Stacey trussed up with cable ties applied to her arms and legs, with a strip of silver Duct Tape covering her mouth.

Ethan produced a knife and quickly cut the restraints and carefully removed the tape so she could breathe freely and take some water from a bottle he had in a backpack. 'You're a sight to behold, Stacey. How are you feeling? Are there any injuries we need to tend to before we try to move you?'

'Oh, I'm so pleased to see you. I was terrified, especially when I saw a snake slither past me, but it was more intent on what I think was a rat which had darted past me. Apart from that, I'm not sure what happened. I feel woozy, which comes and goes and I'm disoriented.' By this time, Letitia appeared with a first aid kit, while Sam and Mitchell fussed over Bailey and Riley for their success in finding Stacey.

'A nasty person ambushed you, injecting you with something to knock you unconscious, which would be the reason you are not feeling too well. You've got a knock at the back of your head that probably happened when you succumbed to the drug that he injected you with, causing you to collapse. Let me put some antiseptic on that head wound and a bandage. We'll phone ahead to the Ranger Station to see if there is some medical help available when we return. You may have a concussion and need to go to a hospital. You're a lucky girl. It could have been so much worse. Something to laugh about with your grandkids one day.'

'Ooh, my head hurts like crazy, so I don't know who's laughing. As for grandkids, I've got to meet *my special someone* first.'

The men took it in turns to carry Stacey back to the ATV's and an hour later they had safely returned to their base. The two police officers who controlled the Drones had surveilled the areas immediately around the cave, but it was clear the kidnapper had long gone. It wasn't long, though, until he contacted Sam via text message.

Nice work copper. I didn't bank on you having the skills of an Aboriginal tracker and sniffer dogs to locate my captive. I was hoping you might not find her and wild animals or lack of water would take its toll. From a distance, I could see you through binoculars. Ho-hum. Who will my next target be? Look after that pretty little female friend of yours. See you, mug copper.

While the park Rangers waited with Stacey until the medical person arrived to check her out, the rest of the rescue group gathered around the conference table to plan their next move. Sam opened the discussion by first reading out the contents of the text he received. Ethan was the first to put forward his ideas.

'That guy sounds really cocky. What he doesn't realise is that he is in our territory now. This is the land of our First Nations people, the Bidjara, Karingbal and

Kara Kara tribes. Nothing happens without us fellas knowing about it. I'll get the message around to all the elders. We'll see how smart he is in trying to evade the custodians of this country, especially when he makes veiled threats about my daughter, Letitia. Will you and your men be sticking around, Russell?'

'Most of us need to get back to Emerald for other matters, but I'll leave my two colleagues who control the Drones. Their expertise could be helpful to your elders. I know they have special tracking skills, similar to what you displayed today, but new technology might just add to their abilities. I'll keep in touch and wish you success.'

'Thanks for your help, Russell. Mitchell and I will now get the message out to our fellow First Nations Leaders. We'll get back to you all tomorrow.'

Chapter Eight

Russell Hoffman's police contingent hadn't been gone more than a half hour when Ranger Stacey fainted, taking a turn for the worse. Letitia quickly leapt into action to check her vital signs and resuscitate her. After a few minutes, she regained consciousness, but her skin was clammy and her breathing laboured.

'I don't think we can wait for a medical person to arrive to check Stacey,' advised Letitia. 'We need to get her to a hospital as soon as possible. With your permission Mr. Moss, I think Sam and I should take off with Stacey immediately for Emerald hospital. She may need a head scan to determine if there is anything more serious.'

'Yes, yes, go. Take as long as you need. Stay with Stacey until she is ready to return. It's probably good that you are not around here, as you appear to be a target for this unknown villain who has wrought havoc in our peaceful environment.'

Letitia made Stacey comfortable in the back seat and sat with her so she could talk to her and keep her conscious for the entire journey. Sam was normally a cautious driver, but he threw caution to the wind and exceeded the speed limit where it was safe to do so. Travel at night on country roads was normally dangerous, with animals like kangaroos or stray cattle liable to leap out in front of a car. Luckily, they experienced no mishaps and could rush Stacey into the emergency department of the hospital, still conscious but not looking at all healthy. They waited while doctors carried out tests and satisfied themselves Stacey was not in any immediate danger. They needed, however, to monitor her until they were satisfied there were no long-term problems.

They booked into the Emerald hotel where they'd stayed previously and although now past 10.00pm with restaurants closed; they were happy to get the last vacancy, a unit with a single and double bed plus room service and a bottle of wine.

'What a day,' Sam declared. 'Thank goodness we can now relax. I hope you are okay to share a room. I don't think I snore.'

Letitia gave a little chuckle. 'It's not like we're total strangers, Sam. No doubt the day was coming when we were going to become more familiar with each other and our habits. What was it that Humphrey Bogart said in the movie Casablanca, *"I think this is the beginning of a beautiful friendship"?* Actually, when I say *"friendship"*, I think we have moved past that stage, don't you? Anyway, let's eat, drink and be merry.'

They enjoyed their meal and the wine put them into a mellow state. Sam attempted to answer Letitia's query about moving past the friendship stage of their relationship. He looked longingly into her eyes and reached across the table to take her hand in his.

'When we were saying goodbye to Blue and Aimee recently, you expressed how you felt so blessed to have bumped into them and also me that night at Rubyvale. You said it was purely a matter of chance, and that's how it was with me. I had no intention of being there that night until they both took pity on me, saying they didn't want to see me on my own and being lonely. I'd planned to spend time writing a love letter to Chloe as part of the process of trying to come to terms with my grief of losing her so tragically. I remember some famous person once saying that life happens while we're making other plans. Because of the grief we both experienced from the loss of loved ones, we were like rudderless ships floundering around in the dark. In the last letter I wrote to Chloe, I received an answer in which she said she gave me permission to find happiness and love again. So, in answer to your question. Yes, we have moved past the friendship phase, and I definitely think we have the basis for future love and happiness.'

Tears appeared in Letitia's eyes and Sam reached over, gently taking her face between his hands, wiping her cheeks as she touched his fingers and softly kissed them. 'You make me so happy, Sam. I never thought I could love again, but I know I'm beginning to. I would like it if you would hold me in your arms so I can feel your strength and warmth encircling me.'

Letitia led Sam to the double bed where they lay embracing each other and, lulled into a state of peaceful dreams following a hectic day, drifted off to sleep. This was the defining moment when they could both accept it was okay to move on together without the limitations of guilt or of feeling they were unfaithful to the memory of their departed loved ones.

As they walked hand in hand from their car to the hospital next morning, they almost felt they were walking on air, such was the glow of realising they were beginning a future filled with a renewed hope for joy and fulfillment. They made their way to the room where Ranger Stacey was resting, following a series of scans and blood tests. Stacey noticed a change in the happy couple and commented. 'Okay, fess up. What's going on between you two? You look so loved up.'

'What us. No, we're just filled with the joy of life and seeing you looking so much better,' replied Letitia, trying to avert attention away from the real reason for their beaming smiles. 'So, what is the verdict from the doctor?'

'The head scans didn't show any signs of permanent damage, except for the concussion. They have put me on a drip to drain from my system whatever drug I was administered. They are keeping me in for a few days to make sure there are no ongoing repercussions. So, you can go out and have an enjoyable time in each other's company and get more of that *joy of life* that seems to have such a positive effect on you both. If you find out what the actual reason for it is, let me know. I want some of what lights you two up so much.'

'Perhaps we'll share it with you when you are feeling better. In the meantime, we're checking with the police to find out if they have a lead on the person who caused you such pain and injury.'

After leaving Stacey and pleased she would make a full recovery, they enquired from the admissions desk if they had a patient named Bob Cook. He was definitely a patient and was recovering from a serious case of pneumonia. They found Bob propped up in bed, hooked up to drips and monitors. He looked drained and in need of a friendly face. As soon as he saw Sam and Letitia, that mischievous look he usually displayed lit up his face.

'You can't believe how much it means to see you two beautiful people again. You look even more beautiful than what I remember from the past. What's your secret?'

'You old silver-tongued scallywag, Bob. It's great to see you on the mend again. We've got to tell you about Bailey. He's a hero back at the Carnarvon Gorge National Park. He performed another amazing rescue of a young Ranger who a scoundrel abducted. She suffered some injuries and is currently recovering also in this hospital. Another thing I've got to tell you. Bailey has got a girlfriend. He's palled up with Letitia's family's dog, Riley. You might have a battle trying to get him to leave her.'

Bob got a sad look on his face, so Sam quickly put him at ease. "No, I'm just joking, old mate. I'm sure he's as eager to see you as you are to see him.'

'Actually,' Letitia interjected, 'as soon as you are healthy enough to travel, I would like you to come back with me and spend some time with my dad

Ethan and mum Imelda. You and dad would have lots in common and it will give you a chance to recover fully. He's bloody good company and my mum's a terrific cook, so you'll get some fat back on those bones in no time.'

'You know I'm a loner. I like my own company most of the time. But I appreciate your invitation and I look forward to meeting your folks, not to mention Bailey's girlfriend. I'm feeling so much better already. You two are special and you bring warmth to an old man's heart,' said Bob, starting to get misty eyed.

'You're an old softie, you know,' responded Letitia, planting a kiss on his cheek. 'We'll drop in to see you before we leave and find out when you will be fit enough to travel.

Chapter Nine

When Sam and Letitia reported to Senior Constable Russ Hoffman at the Emerald Police Station, Sam informed him of the condition of Ranger Stacey and also that of Bob Cook, affectionately known as *old Bob*. Sam outlined the recent history of phone texts from Stacey's attacker, from the first one he received in Mt. Isa, to those recently in Carnarvon Gorge.

'This guy claims to have some contact with a previous perpetrator I arrested who is blaming me for all he's lost while he was in prison. He says I *arrested one of his brothers*, so it's not clear if the vendetta being carried out on me is on behalf of a direct relative or someone he just refers to as a brother. He also says this brother was recently released from prison. This may be the clue to enable us to get a name and face for who's behind this drama, if indeed it is his blood brother. So, Russ, can you contact the Criminal Investigation Branch, Brisbane, to go through my history of arrests and find out who has come out of jail in the last twelve months? It's probably best to come direct from a serving police officer rather than me because I'm still on leave. It could end up being *a wild goose chase,* but it's worth checking.'

'Good idea Sam. I'll alert them to all that has happened, including the texts you've received. Leave me your phone for a couple of hours and I'll see if the tech guys can access it remotely and determine the source of the texts. They're probably using a burner phone, which is untraceable, but it is worth a try. Why don't you take Letitia to lunch and let me worry about this? There's an Italian place opposite to where you're staying. My wife and I dine there at least once a fortnight. Lorenzo is the owner. Tell him you know me and he'll give you special treatment. I'll ring Letitia in a couple of hours.'

After they arrived at the restaurant and been welcomed in the manner many Italian restauranteurs are renowned for, Sam and Letitia ordered their entrees on the recommendation of Lorenzo and a glass of Franciacorta, better known as *the champagne of Italy* for starters. 'Well, here's to us, my lovely Letitia. This is to celebrate our first official date as a couple,' gestured Sam, clinking his glass against hers.

'That's very nice of you to mark this occasion, my handsome Sam. I will store it in the memory bank of my special moments.' Raising her glass, she continued, 'and here's to all the memories we are going to make together.'

Letitia's phone buzzed with a message from Russell as they were finishing their dessert and the last glass of a bottle of Pinot Noir, the gift from Lorenzo. He made this generous gesture after they shared with him they were on their first official date as a couple. 'So wonderful to share this special moment. Buona Fortuna, you are a beautiful couple,' said Lorenzo.

On their return, Russell greeted them, commenting on how happy they looked as they walked into the police station, holding hands. 'Looks like it was a great lunch from the glow on your faces. A great experience or just the effects of the wine.'

'Mostly a great experience. Maybe a little from the wine,' commented Sam. 'So, anything good to report?'

'Regarding identifying perpetrators you've put in prison who have been released in the past twelve months. You have a choice of three, which probably doesn't narrow it down a lot. We have their names and mug shots, so it may assist further down the track. The phone, as we suspected, is a burner phone, so no help with that. I got an update from the two officers I left down at Carnarvon. They've coordinated with your father and brother. There doesn't appear to be any movement yet of strangers in the Carnarvon Gorge or its immediate surrounds. They have put the word out through the Indigenous network and local businesses, particularly hotels, motels, fuel stations and food outlets, to report to them any strangers they think might not be a genuine visitor or are acting suspiciously. We'll just have to wait and see. Sorry, I didn't have better news. Here's your phone Sam. When are you heading back?'

'Probably tomorrow. Ranger Stacey should be fit enough to travel after the doctors give her all clear,' replied Sam. 'A couple of other things I should have asked you to check up for me, Russ. There should be two Court cases coming up that I will need to attend to give evidence. One is in Brisbane to deal with that grub, Jimmy Johnson, who killed Chloe and the other will be in Townsville to deal with Curly Jacobs and Charlie Briggs, those mongrels responsible for kidnapping me and abandoning me to die on a deserted island in the Gulf of Carpentaria. Mitchell might have to be involved in the Townsville one also as he worked undercover, that helped provide the information which led to their capture for cattle rustling. I'd appreciate that, mate. I'll call before we head back to Carnarvon.'

After they left the police station, Sam had an idea to fill in a couple of hours. 'While we have time, I thought we might take a tour out to Fairbairn Dam. It is the lifeblood for the town and the farmers in the region. We can stick around to see the sunset. First, though, we can take a stroll through the Emerald Botanic Gardens on the way.' This was just a simple pleasure but meandering through a tropical paradise and oasis located hundreds of kilometres inland from the coast had a special feeling as they walked hand in hand.

By the time they reached Fairbairn Dam, the sun was setting. The sky changed colour with each passing minute. The low-floating clouds were a palette of bright orange, pink and gold as they changed colours, stretching across the horizon until the fiery red disc of the sun disappeared behind the distant hills. 'That is breathtaking,' whispered Letitia as she kissed Sam.

It was a lingering kiss, evoking the excitement of participating in a memorable experience and a feeling of happiness which neither of them wished to end. They remained in a loving embrace, with the silvery orb of the moon replacing the round red sun, which had created such passion and awakened their deeper senses. They felt so thrilled with the joy of each other's company that it seemed they walked and talked for hours as the night sky delighted with its shimmering panorama of stars that hung like a massive tapestry, the work of a master artist.

'I can never get enough of the beauty of the night skies with their array of stars. It is more spectacular here in the outback, with no pollution to mask its magnificence,' enthused Letitia. 'It just makes the experience so much more special. I feel truly blessed, especially as I am sharing it with you.'

'Talking of stars, you know *the Milky Way* has special significance for our Aboriginal ancestors and is common in Aboriginal languages. That's why I named mine and Chloe's unborn son Waru, because in Kalkadoon country, the land of my ancestors, the term Waru is used to describe *the Milky Way*. Whenever I look up at the night sky, I can feel as though they are present, like stars shining down on me. It gives me strength to keep going. It is my way of celebrating their presence in my life.'

'Oh, my dear Sam. I know exactly how you feel. You are giving me some of that strength now, for being with you has helped me feel alive again after the loss and grief I also experienced. I'm glad you told me about the meaning of your son's name. Although I never met Chloe, I believe her love is shining down on us. It is indeed the feeling of *love under the Milky Way*.'

'What a beautiful way of putting it, Letitia. I am so happy it is helping you and will now be something that will have such an important bearing on our life together.'

'Thanks for such a memorable moment in our lives and may there be a lifetime of them?', affirmed Letitia as they lovingly made their way back to Emerald, enveloped in a glow of boundless hope for the future.

Chapter Ten

Sam and Letitia's growing affection for each other meant that each moment they shared was another opportunity for their relationship to grow and gradually emerge from the dark mists of grief that had overshadowed their thoughts and feelings since the tragic events that shattered their lives. They had known joy and happiness and love and, in their hearts, they believed achieving that again would mostly lift the overpowering shadow of the past loss and grief from their future. The new love that was appearing, however, felt different and as they sat in their room now, sharing a light meal together, Letitia turned the conversation to what this meant as they moved forward into a more peaceful place.

'Sam, you will soon leave to attend the court cases you spoke to Russell Hoffman about. I know we have only known each other for a relatively short time, but I think what has happened to both of us is what is binding us together. This feeling I am experiencing, I believe, is the start of love and I want to see that grow. It feels different from what I felt for Michael, but having lost someone I've loved means they still share a part of who I am. I want you to know, though, that I still have plenty of love to give and hope to share. When you are far away in Brisbane and Townsville, please be aware I will think about you constantly, every day.'

'Letitia, I couldn't have expressed how I feel any better. You have such an amazing insight and depth of understanding. Like you mentioned with Michael, I know Chloe will always be a part of me. That is the respect that we each have for them and their memory. I want us always to be free to talk about our feelings including those for our departed partners. That is the basis on which lasting love will grow and, like you, I know love has found a way into my life again. One thing I've learnt from my loss of Chloe is not to take anything for granted and value each moment. Thanks to technology, it is easy these days to keep the flame of love shining bright and I will talk to you each day I'm away on FaceTime.'

Love enveloped them that night as they held each other close, passionately kissing and blissfully falling into a deep sleep to dream of their future as a united couple.

******

Ranger Stacey had received confirmation from the doctors she was fit to return to Carnarvon, but to take a week off before returning to duty. When Sam and Letitia arrived, Stacey was eagerly waiting, relieved as most people are to not spend more time than necessary in a hospital. They also called to see *old Bob* and assure him they would be in touch to arrange for him to come and stay with Letitia's family so he could recuperate before attempting to resume his mining ventures.

Driving into Carnarvon Gorge always generated an exhilarating feeling, which Sam observed in Letitia and Stacey, mirrored in their clear look of delight. 'Anyone would think you missed the place,' commented Sam, as a smile lit up both of their faces.

They were soon at the Wilderness Lodge to the welcoming embraces of staff, friends, and guests who had been concerned for Stacey's wellbeing. Among the guests were Letitia's father, Ethan, and her brother Mitchell. As everyone was breaking up into little groups, it became appropriate for Letitia's purposes that she, Stacey, and Mitchell were together while Ethan and Sam were talking to other people.

'Stacey, I don't think you've met my big brother, Mitch. He was my protector growing up, making sure I didn't get into too much trouble. Now I've got someone else to care for me in Sam. That means Mitchell is a free man to be a protector of someone else. After that scare with your abduction recently, you may have a need for a real he-man to protect you. I can certainly vouch for his effectiveness. There's been nights when we've been out and about at a football function or a country dance when some guy becomes a nuisance and Mitch has gently persuaded him that his health could be in danger if he persisted. Well, not so much in those terms. Probably a bit more direct, *like piss off dickhead if you know what's good for you.*'

'Yeah, that's me,' said Mitch, 'muscle for hire, especially if it involves a pretty girl.' Letitia made the excuse of needing to go to the restroom, leaving nature to take its course with the newly introduced couple.

Meanwhile, Sam and Ethan found themselves on their own, which gave Sam the opportunity to have a talk with Letitia's father concerning where Sam's relationship with his daughter was heading. 'No doubt Letitia has spoken to you about me, and I need you to know that we are becoming very fond of each other. You would also know that we have both suffered from the loss of our partners because of the criminal acts of others. This was something that initially gave us a united bond and brought us consolation. We could lean on each other for support. It has gone way past that point now, I am pleased to say. We are now more than just friends and I think we can see ourselves down the track in a permanent relationship. I have to go away to give evidence in two court cases soon, but I want you to know I'll be back. I just needed you to know that I'm genuine about your daughter.'

Slapping Sam firmly on his back in a confirming manner, Ethan replied, 'When you say Letitia may have talked about you. Hell, Sam, she doesn't bloody well talk much about anything else. You make an old man extremely happy hearing you talk so affectionately about his daughter because she talks about you in the same way. She took it hard when Michael was killed, and I didn't know if she'd ever surface from that dark place in her mind. I feel she is now back to what she used to be like, happy with a smile on her face, always there for anyone wanting help or support. You have done that for her, Sam. You have my deep admiration. She'll be safe in our hands while you're away. If your relationship develops into a more permanent thing, know that you have the blessing of me an Imelda.'

'Phew,' said Sam with a pretend wipe across his brow. 'I thought that might be more harrowing than it was. Thanks for understanding and putting me at ease. Now, what's happening with that mongrel who's causing us so much concern? For my peace of mind, I'd like to see the bloke locked up before I head off to Brisbane.'

'Mitchell and I have arranged a meeting tomorrow morning with the leaders of the Indigenous tribes around and including Carnarvon Gorge. We've got a few clues about where he may possibly hang out. If you'd like to come along, we'd appreciate your input from your experience as a detective with the Queensland police. Our mob and the other tribes like nothing more than a hunt for rogue animals. More to prevent them from causing harm to others. We'll stay in a cabin nearby tonight and pick you up first thing in the morning.'

'Thanks for that. You're a wise man. I'll be ready by 7.00am. Let's hope for a rewarding hunt.'

Leaving Ethan to round up Mitchell, Sam found Letitia ready to call it a night so they could head to her cabin together. She had put her arm around his waist, heading for the door when Ranger Stacey rushed up beside Letitia. 'So, I'm inquisitive. What was that all about, introducing me to your very handsome brother, then disappearing, leaving us alone? Not that I minded. We got on really well. In fact, he has invited me out next weekend.'

'Well, there you go. My mission here is accomplished. When we visited you in hospital in Emerald, you remarked you wanted *some of what lights us two up so much*. Mitch is a single red blooded Aussie bloke. You're a single woman with qualities I know will excite him. What more can I say? The rest is up to you. Good night. Sweet dreams and have a wonderful date with a man who deserves someone as wonderful as you.' Letitia departed as a mischievous smile filled her face and she cheekily winked at Stacey.

Chapter Eleven

Sam, Ethan and Mitchell gathered with the leaders of each of the First Nations communities on whose land the Carnarvon Gorge and surrounding areas were located. Also in attendance were police officers, Davies and Price, who specialised in operating the aerial surveillance afforded by the drones. Ethan led the discussion by asking if there had been any sighting of the suspect responsible for the abduction of Ranger Stacey and the threats to Sam and Letitia. The elder representing the rest of the leaders spoke first.

'On one cattle station on the southern boundary of the Gorge, the owner contacted us. He said they were mustering cattle by helicopter in a remote part of their property and the pilot reported he saw a man skulking about a cabin that was only used when the stockmen were out doing maintenance on the fences. He said nobody from the station had been sent to do that. It might be worth checking out.'

They estimated it would take a couple of hours over extremely rough terrain in places to reach the suspect area by four-wheel-drives. Those men at the meeting all had suitable vehicles. They worked on arriving about midday.

The area surrounding the location of the cabin was extremely heavily forested, which meant they had to proceed on foot for about half a kilometre. The police officers suggested they get closer but not be observed. His plan was to send up their drones to get an idea of what they might expect before taking any risks. With the two drone operators leading the group along a well-worn path, they had only gone about one hundred metres when a flash and a loud bang resulted in the lead police officer falling to the ground. Everyone ducked for cover initially before running to the aid of officer Davies. He had been wearing a bullet-proof vest and the shotgun blast did not hit him with full force, only partially hitting the vest, and knocking him to the ground. Mostly he was shocked and winded, with a minimum number of pellets hitting his arm. As they checked the officer's wounds, they heard either a motor bike or an ATV roaring off into the distance.

'The bastard,' cussed Ethan. 'He must have set up a booby trap with a trip wire to warn him of anyone approaching. So, he'll now be up on two charges, kidnapping and attempted murder of a police officer.' They returned to their vehicles where officer Davies was treated for the obvious wounds to his right arm. One of the Indigenous leaders volunteered to drive officer Davies back to receive further treatment while the others would try to pick up the direction their suspect was headed. Ethan had his satellite phone with him and immediately contacted the owner of the station.

'Hi Harry,' greeted Ethan, then explained in detail what had happened. 'Would it be possible for you to have your helicopter pilot take a look around and see if he can spot this character? We must stop him before he hurts anyone else. You'll need to be careful, though. He might decide to take a pot shot at your chopper. He looked to be headed north. We'll head in that direction and as soon as you locate him, just keep him in your sights and we'll try to catch up.'

'Sure thing, Ethan. We'll head him off and let you know when we have him in our sights.'

'Okay,' officer Price commented. 'If Harry is successful and our suspect is armed and starts shooting at us, I can put up my drone to see his hiding place so I can work out how to best deal with his capture. How many of you have a weapon?'

They all advised they had a rifle, which they normally used to hunt feral pigs and wild dogs that attacked their cattle. 'If we trap him and he sees we have superior firepower, I hope I can get him to surrender. We're too isolated to call for backup, so it will be a matter of needing to stop him the best way possible. If he tries shooting his was out, we'll have no alternative but to return fire.'

They had been travelling about thirty minutes when Harry phoned Ethan to advise him they had spotted someone driving an ATV and were on its trail. He gave Ethan directions to catch up. 'I don't think he checked out the country too much before he chose this place to use as a hideout. He's headed up a valley that is a dead end. I'll get the pilot to drop me and my son off about half a kilometre from where your suspect can't proceed any further. We'll take cover behind some boulders. We're both armed, so he can't escape. I'll send the chopper back to guide you into the valley.'

There were five vehicles in the convoy that arrived and spread out across the width of the valley to present an imposing sight for the trapped aggressor they would try to convince to surrender peacefully. The first plan of action was to launch the drone to identify his exact location. The drone hovered around using the thermal imaging camera on board to locate the suspect amongst some trees. Just as officer Price was getting the loud hailer to tell the hiding man to surrender, there were several gunshots which hit the drone. It crashed to the ground in a ball of flame. Shortly after, there was a tirade of swearing and a challenge to, '*try to take me alive, yah mongrels. Anyone approaches, I'll kill them.*' Officer Price sent up a second drone but kept it at a safe distance and then got onto the loud hailer.

'Whoever you are, you have no chance of escape. If you attempt to use your weapon to fire in our direction, we will have no option but to retaliate. We are in no hurry. We can wait here for as long as it takes for you to either come to your senses or do something stupid.' To conserve the drone's batteries, the officer brought it back to earth.

No sooner had he finished speaking than several bullets fired from a rifle ricocheted off one of the vehicles. This meant they had no option but to out-wait the aggressor. It wasn't long before the sun set and darkness enveloped the valley. In case the suspect thought he could sneak past them under cover of night, officer Price deployed the drone again. It's thermal imaging camera and night-vision lens quickly picked up movement which they could see on an iPad screen. The movement was amongst the trees lined along one side of the valley. Officer Price, along with Ethan and Mitchell, moved to where the suspect was heading and lay in wait. When he was next to their position, Price and Mitchell leapt out simultaneously before he could fire his rifle. Mitchell was a big man who'd spent plenty of time wrangling wild bush cattle, physically bringing them to the ground with his practiced technique. The villain struggled and landed a glancing blow to the side of Mitchell's face, which was a mistake. Not only was Mitchell a wild cattle wrangler, but he had also been the Central Queensland heavyweight boxing champion. A well-aimed left to the solar plexus knocked the air from his lungs, followed by a pile driving uppercut punch to the chin, knocking him unconscious.

Officer Price put the man in handcuffs and he and Mitchell carried him back to where the others were waiting. One man produced some smelling salts that were placed under the unconscious man's nose, quickly reviving him. Officer Price read him his rights before arresting him for kidnap, attempted murder, destruction of police property (i.e. the drone and bullet-holed car) plus the promise of several other possible charges once he had time to fully evaluate his crimes. They were all pleased with the outcome and were looking forward to getting back home to check on the condition of officer Davies.

Chapter Twelve

When Sam, Ethan and Mitchell walked into the Ranger Station at Carnarvon Gorge National Park, there was a collective sigh of relief with news the kidnapper of Ranger Stacey was in custody. The manager greeted them with the good news that police officer Davies had mostly superficial wounds but with the likelihood of needing a Xray to determine if there were any lead pellets needing to be removed.

Letitia engaged Stacey in conversation to ask how she was recovering after her ordeal but couldn't help making a comment about her brother Mitchell and his valiant effort in ambushing Stacey's assailant. 'You should ask Mitch about how he captured the prisoner. He's too modest to take any credit. He's kind of the strong, silent type who doesn't talk about himself. I'm sure you'll discover many great things about him if you ask other people. You can tell I'm a proud sister.' Stacey thanked her and said she would show her appreciation for his bravery.

Before Senior Constable Russ Hoffman departed with the prisoner, Sam spoke with him.

'I'm thinking, Russ, that I'd like to be there when you question our suspect to find out firstly who he is but also who the brother is he refers to who appears to have a vendetta against me. There might be word back also about when I need to attend the Court case in Brisbane for Chloe's killer. It would be helpful to know who might stalk me while I'm there.'

'I can't see a problem with that, Sam. You can observe from the room with the two-way glass and relay any questions or concerns you have through an earpiece I'll wear.'

'Great, I'll go pack some things quickly and follow you. I'd say *old Bob* should be about ready to be released from hospital, so I'll be able to bring him back to recuperate with Letitia's family and his best mate, Bailey.'

Letitia accompanied Sam back to their cabin for a quick hello and goodbye. 'I'll certainly be able to breathe easier without having to keep looking behind my back for someone trying to accost me,' a relieved Letitia commented. 'He hasn't obviously talked yet and given the police his name. Do you think you'll find out more details to help you be prepared when you're in Brisbane attending your court case? I'm worried there are others out to hurt you. I'll be a nervous wreck until it's all over.'

'If he doesn't share that information, I guess the next thing will be to match his fingerprints and DNA profile with the databases in the police system. He says it's, *one of our brothers,* who he was acting on behalf of, so it's possible there's a link. I'm puzzled by the, *our brothers,* reference, though.'

'Here's hoping you are successful. Let me know if *old Bob* is coming back with you so we can prepare a welcome. I'm sure he'll be looking forward to being out and about again with his best mate, Bailey.' With that, Letitia took Sam into her arms, passionately kissing him, while whispering in his ear how much she'd miss him.

'I'll miss you too, you sexy lady,' he whispered back.

'Wow, sexy lady now. I like that, my big hunk of sexy man.' They clung to each other for several minutes, not wanting to part as each time they did, they felt more the loneliness of the separation.

******

Next day, Sam breezed into the Emerald Police station at the time he'd prearranged with Russell for the interview with their *no name prisoner*. Senior Sergeant Matt Ogilvie, along with Senior Constable Russell Hoffman, conducted the interview, while Sam was a passive observer in the adjoining room, from where he could see everything happening.

'Interview with uncooperative respondent started at 10.00am. Sir, we have advised you of your rights,' then Matt went through the procedure of informing the prisoner they were being recorded by in-house video. 'Now, at this stage, you are refusing to inform us of your name. 'Is there any reason that is the case?'

'No comment,' he replied.

'We have charged you initially with the serious crimes of kidnapping with violence, administering an illegal substance to stun your victim, attempted murder of a police officer, possession of a firearm without a license and discharging said firearm, plus assault of one of your captors. We have both photo and video evidence to support most of the charges. There is also the matter of a threatening letter you left on the vehicle of Detective Sergeant Mackenzie, in Mt. Isa, and subsequent threatening text messages sent to his phone. These have been entered into evidence as well. These are all very serious charges. Is there anything you wish to say on your behalf?'

'No comment,' he replied.

'Seeing you are presenting as being uncooperative in answering our questions, you are required to submit to fingerprinting and supplying a DNA sample. Do you understand?'

'Yeah, you can bloody well try,' he replied. At this stage, the respondent became very agitated, and the interviewer advised him that additional restraints would be applied to him, such as being chained to the table or the administration of a sedative in order for tests to be carried out.

'Mr. Whatever your name is. It's not about asking for your agreement. We are in our rights to employ whatever means necessary to carry out those two tasks. You can do it the easy way or you can do it the hard way. It doesn't matter to us. It's your choice.'

'One further thing we will then proceed with after your prints and DNA,' added Russell, 'is to contact the media outlets in Mt. Isa, providing them with your photo to circulate to the community and inquire if anyone can provide us with your identity. You think you're smart, but this is not the first time we've encountered an uncooperative respondent. When we find out your name, we'll then try to identify who the brother you refer to is who's planned a vendetta against DS Mackenzie.'

'Haven't you ever heard the expression, *he's got a brother from another father'*, the respondent smirked. 'Good luck with that.'

'You obviously don't know a lot about DNA profiles. We'll be able to determine if there is a relationship between you and *the brother* you referred to in your letter attached to DS Mackenzie's car, if your mother is the same.'

'You don't know if I was referring to an actual blood brother. It could all be a smokescreen. I could have meant *a brother in arms or a brother for a cause.* You'll have to wait and see.'

'So, another threat. Interview finished at 11.05am,' concluded Officer Ogilvie.

******

After they returned the prisoner to the lock-up, Sam met up with Russell Hoffman, who asked. 'What did you think of the response from the respondent? He sure seemed cock-sure of himself.'

'The way he carried on, I don't think he has much respect for the police or regard for law and order. I won't be surprised when you learn his name, that you'll find he has a criminal record. I'm at a quandary regarding what he meant by his reference to *a brother in arms or a brother for a cause.* Anyhow, if I worry about it, he'll have succeeded in making me fearful.

What have you found out about when I need to travel to Brisbane for the Jimmy Johnson trial?'

'The trial date's set for next Monday week. It's suggested you are available to speak to the prosecution during the previous week. I've checked on flights and I've made a booking for you with Virgin airlines departing this Friday at 5.00pm. Does that suit?'

'Thanks for that Russ. I'm happy with that. That gives me time to pick up *old Bob* from hospital and take him back to Carnarvon with me, get him settled in with Letitia's family and enjoy their company for a few days. I'll check in with you next Friday.'

Sam had rung the hospital when he arrived in Emerald and had learned that Bob was ready to be discharged. Bob was prancing around his room when Sam arrived. 'Looks like you're eager to make tracks. What, you didn't enjoy your stay?'

A few nurses appeared at the door before Bob could answer. 'Ah, you're not taking our favourite patient. He's a bit of a loveable larrikin, you know. He brightened up our day with his wild bush stories and outback humour. We'll miss you, Bob,' they chorused and with that embraced him in a group hug.

'Oh, stop it ladies. You'll start me crying soon and ruin my reputation as a tough old bastard.'

They accompanied him to the front doors and waved him goodbye as the car took off for the journey to Carnarvon and his old mate, Bailey, his blue heeler dog and best friend.

Chapter Thirteen

The love of a man for his dog and vice versa is best displayed when they have been separated for some time and are reunited again. Such was the case with *old Bob* and his best mate, Bailey. As soon as he hopped out of the car, Bailey came bounding towards him, leaping up at Bob, almost knocking him over. 'Ah, what a sight for sore eyes. Just look at you, you've never looked so healthy. They must be feeding you some *good tucker*, or is it this little lady over here I've been hearing so much about that's put a spring in your step? So, this is your girlfriend, you sly dog. She's looking healthy too. What's your secret Letitia?'

'Well, about that Bob. Riley's put on some weight, but not so much from eating some *good tucker*. I believe there's going to be several extra mouths to feed in the not-too-distant future. It seems Bailey and Riley have been doing more that chasing criminals. They're going to be parents. What do you think about that?'

'Well, stone the bloody crows. You scallywag Bailey. What a wonderful surprise!' With that, Bob embraced each dog in a big hug.

'Bob, I'd like you to meet my mom and dad, Imelda, and Ethan. You'll be in their loving hands until you feel you are healthy enough to return to your home. Just like Bailey, I'm sure they will fatten you up and return you to full fitness. This here is my brother Mitchell, and we thought you'd like to meet the young lady that Bailey and Riley tracked down and saved recently. This is Stacey, who works as a Ranger at Carnarvon Gorge National Park.'

Stacey stepped up to thank Bob with a friendly kiss and a hug. 'I've heard the stories about Bailey saving your life, Bob. Now I've joined the select group of his rescues. He's such a special dog. I hope his offspring follows in his footsteps.'

'Well, Ethan's dog Riley also played a part, I hear. Depending on how many pups they have in their litter, perhaps you might be lucky and score one of them. They're the best friend and protector you can get. Unless the big strapping bloke beside you fills those roles.'

With that, Ethan extended the welcome of his family to Bob. 'I'd be more than happy for Stacey to have one of their pups and the big strapping bloke is my son, Mitchell. From my observation, he and Stacey are very compatible and happy together. I'm looking forward to chatting with you, Bob. The Gemfields used to be where I did a bit of mining years ago. No doubt you've got plenty of tall tales to tell.' Everybody then gathered around to make Bob welcome.

Letitia was not only pleased with the way her family responded to Bob's company, but also with how they embraced Stacey. She also felt a glow of inner joy and accomplishment seeing Stacey and Mitchell walking arm in arm together.

This was the first time Sam had spent any time with Letitia and her entire family. She surprised him with an introduction to another sister and brother but also extended family who gathered for this family get together. He felt so much closer now, knowing he was accepted into such a loving and united family circle.

The family home was a rambling and spacious building along the lines of most properties on outback cattle stations, which, from time to time, catered to large groups of family and friends. Plenty of bedrooms and makeshift camp beds on the verandas surrounding the main house. The family celebrations continued into the night, with most allocated to separate sleeping quarters. A few had their pop-up camper trailers, which were popular when visiting family members scattered far and wide in a country as big as Australia.

Eventually, when they were alone in their room, and with everyone settled down for the night, Sam brought Letitia up to date with what had eventuated from the interview with Stacey's kidnapper.

'So, is there anything I need to worry about concerning your safety while you're down in Brisbane?'

'We hope to know more about any likely threats from *his so-called brother,* which he referred to in his Mt. Isa letter. The police in Emerald have taken his fingerprints and DNA to find out any family contacts.' Sam didn't purposely mention about the respondent's reference made to *a brother in arms or a brother for a cause,* as he didn't want to alarm her more than necessary.

'Let's not concern ourselves with things that might never happen,' advised Sam. 'For the next few days, I just want to enjoy being with you and feeling the love that is growing between us.'

'Oh Sam. At this moment, I have never felt so close to anyone as I am now to you, my darling. Come here, my big strapping man and protector.' With that, they melted into each other's arms and kissed passionately.

Separating slightly after several minutes, Letitia looked lovingly into Sam's eyes. 'It means so much to be here with you in my family home where I grew up and where I have so many beautiful memories. Being with you now makes my story feel almost complete. It would mean so much to me to complete my love story with you at this moment, in this place. I want you to make love to me, Sam, for a memory that will last a lifetime.' They again melted into each other's arms and with passion rising to heights they were now reaching for the first time, their bodies merged as one as, in unison, they reached the ultimate climax together that a couple in complete love can ever achieve with intense ecstasy stimulating their senses.

As Letitia rolled over on top of Sam, staring deeply into his eyes and with the afterglow of passion lighting up her face, she kissed him and whispered in his ear. 'While you're away and we hook up on FaceTime, the memory of what we have shared will be forefront in my thoughts and I will feel as though I am there with you.' They remained embracing as one while drifting off into a state of release and freedom only experienced when couples fully unite in sexual passion for the first time.

Chapter Fourteen

The next three days were special in terms of their relationship as Sam and Letitia strove to reinforce and build on their love that had blossomed and grown from the most unlikely of circumstances, namely the tragic death of both their partners. They had sought refuge from their pain and grief initially by supporting each other. This turned to friendship, followed by a mutual attraction which ignited a flame, diminishing the darkness cast by the loss of their loved ones. Each moment now was precious. They had only days before their unwelcome separation brought about by Sam's necessary attendance at two criminal trials, first in Brisbane, followed by another in Townsville.

'Oh Sam, last night was so beautiful. I can't explain how meaningful it is to know that our love is now complete.' As Letitia was affirming her feelings, tears glistened in her eyes, reflecting the joy she experienced.

'I never thought I'd ever feel so much in love again,' reinforced Sam, wiping away her tears. 'Intimacy was the last barrier to achieving complete love and now we are there, it can only grow stronger. Distance can't separate us, neither can any obstacles that life throws at us. We can weather any storm now that we are completely united.'

They filled their remaining days with passionate lovemaking that did not have the urgency of their first union. Now their time was more about finding the things that made their experience more fulfilling and joyful, ensuring that each reached the highest peak of ecstasy whenever they were intimate. Alas, Friday arrived too soon, and Sam and Letitia felt sadness about being separated. Sam consoled Letitia when their last kiss released more tears flowing down her cheeks. Cradling her face in his hands, he softly kissed away her tears as he whispered, 'I love you. I love you. I love you,' to emphasise and reinforce to her his commitment. As his car slowly pulled away, he couldn't help but feel a wrenching in his heart as he saw Letitia in his rear-view mirror, still dabbing tears from her eyes.

******

The first thing that Senior Constable Russ Hoffman said on observing him arriving at Emerald Police station was, 'Why so sad, Sam? I thought you'd be looking forward to catching up with your fellow police officers in Brisbane.'

'Let's just say I'd feel a lot happier if it didn't mean being separated from Letitia. I'm sure you understand, being in love with your beautiful wife. That's how my love for Letitia has blossomed. Grief bought us together, and we have realised so much more the depth of our feelings for each other in recent days.

So much so that it is sad to be apart from her, if that makes sense.'

'I know exactly what you mean, Sam. If it's any consolation, *absence does make the heart grow fonder*. Excuse the cliché. I'm so happy for you both that you have found love again. I know it must have been hard knowing how much you loved Chloe. I'm sure she would understand that life goes on. Anyway, I've got you booked into a one-bedroom apartment at Meriton Suites, Herschel Street, Brisbane. It's walking distance to both the Magistrates' Courts and the Police Headquarters. I wasn't sure if you've arranged transport from the airport.'

'No, that's fine. I rang Chloe's mum and dad before I got here and they will pick me up. Have you had any result from the fingerprints or DNA you took from the guy we interviewed?'

'We haven't got any DNA results yet, but the fingerprints brought up a record for a perp by the name of Reece Roberts who has previous criminal charges, namely for selling drugs, robbery with violence and threats with a knife. He has a brother who has a family and never been in trouble with the police. So, reference to *a brother in arms or a brother for a cause* could mean he has connections to a gang or to bikies. Your mates in the CIB might be able to shed more light on that.' Russell drove Sam to the airport and waited until he boarded and the flight departed.

On arrival in Brisbane, Sybil and Brian McCarthy, Chloe's parents, greeted him with the affection he had always shared with them. 'Great to see you guys again. How are you coping?'

'I guess you know, Sam, it never ends, the grief,' shared Sybil. 'We find it's getting easier with time and our other daughter and son with their children make the burden lighter. I've also set up that foundation in Chloe's name that I mentioned to you at her funeral. That has been a watershed in helping Chloe's death be meaningful to help abused women. We are having a rally next week before the trial for her killer. I arranged it to have maximum effect, relating to the trial and hopeful sentencing of Jimmy Johnson. We never got around to thanking you for your bravery and persistence in bringing him to justice. That has helped both of us also, so we are deeply thankful to you, Sam.'

'Thanks for coming to pick me up. We can talk some more when we get to my apartment. If you haven't eaten yet, I'm sure we can order in some food and catch up. I've got a lot to share and I want to hear more about Chloe's foundation.'

When they'd arrived and could sit and relax, Sam found a menu in the compendium of information and ordered a variety of Chinese dishes to share.

After they had eaten and were enjoying a glass of wine, Sam felt it appropriate to address the delicate topic of his newfound love with Letitia.

'You both know how much I loved Chloe and still do. She was my soulmate and I'll be honest, there were times when the grief of her passing was overwhelming.

So much so that I needed some help from a person trained in dealing with the loss of a loved one.'

Sam described the process by which he could reach out to Chloe and express in the form of a love letter his feelings and how he missed her. He shared with them how it worked and also showed them the letters he wrote to Chloe and those he believed were her replies. 'I can't explain how it happens, but it has brought so much peace into my heart. I feel she and our unborn son are in a happy place.' They spent some time reading through the letters, with Sybil becoming misty eyed when she finished.

'Thanks for sharing that, Sam. Reading your letters to each other also brings peace and happiness to us,' shared Brian. 'I believe it is best not to question the process, but to be thankful for the outcome.'

'I want to share with you something else that happened to me on my journey back to accepting life is worth living again. By chance or by circumstance, I met a young woman who had experienced similar grief to mine when her future husband was killed by one of those coward punch incidents that have become more prevalent these days. I shared with her how she might address her grief by writing love letters to her lost love. She also found a peace of mind similar to what I experienced and has now become involved in a *one punch kills* foundation. It's like the one you have set up to address domestic violence, which led indirectly to Chloe's death. Recently, I joined her at a *one punch kills* rally in Mt. Isa to share her story and alert people to the futility of expressing anger through violence.'

'It sounds like you have found a companion traveller. We totally think it is wonderful you're able to help each other in a common cause,' assured Sybil.

'While we have been supporting each other, we have developed feelings I believe to be love. I want to be up front now because you may think it is inappropriate that I have found a person I am attracted to who you may feel is a replacement for Chloe. I can only say that I didn't intentionally go looking for love so soon after losing Chloe. Call it fate, I don't know, but it was completely unexpected and unplanned, as it was for her. I only hope it doesn't upset you both.'

'My dear boy,' consoled Sybil. 'We knew eventually you would find someone else to love, which is only natural. The fact it is sooner rather than later is immaterial. What matters is that you are both happy and can find peace together. I note in Chloe's last letter to you she wished for you to find love again. So, she gave you her blessing, and so do we. We hope to meet your lady friend whenever you feel the time is right. Tell us more about her?' Sam obliged by explaining how he met Letitia, what she did for a living, the close ties she has with family and the fact she was like him, a First Nations person.

Both Sybil and Brian lifted their glasses in a toast. 'Here's wishing the best for you and Letitia, Sam. We wish you both happiness. We look forward to having her in our family and from what you have told us about her, she will be as dear to us as you are. Now, you mentioned how you helped Letitia when she spoke at her rally about the effects of the coward punch program. Could I impose on you to be involved with our rally on domestic violence this coming Thursday? I'm sure your account of the trauma and grief you experienced when Chloe died attending a domestic violence incident will touch people's hearts.'

'That would be both a pleasure and privilege to help you and to make the loss of Chloe a positive influence for abused women. Thanks for accepting Letitia and understanding the love that has helped us both through the worst time in our lives. You are both such understanding people and I love you like my own parents. I'll see you Friday.' With that, they joined in a group hug before departing.

Chapter Fifteen

'I know it's not a day yet since you left, Sam, but I'm so missing you already,' were Letitia's first words when she answered his call. 'Did everything go as planned with your travel and meeting Chloe's parents for the first time since her passing?'

'Yes, I'm all settled into the apartment Russell booked for me. Likewise, I'm missing you too. I've got to tell you about Sybil and Brian. They have been fantastic. I was very tentative about telling them of our relationship, but they rationalised by saying it would happen eventually and they weren't concerned it had happened so soon. I pointed out that it was more by chance than anything planned. They were so caring and understanding and guess what, they want to meet you? I hope you don't mind, but I gave them your phone number. They said they would love to reach out and make you feel welcome.'

'Wow, I don't know. I would be so nervous I wouldn't know what to talk about.'

'No, in all sincerity, they would make you feel at ease as soon as you talked to them. They asked me all about you, so they know already that you are a wonderful person. I also told them how we shared our grief because of what had happened so they can empathise with you because of their own grief. I informed them of how you also shared your story of the loss of Michael at the *one punch kills* rally and how I supported you through that. Sybil has a similar rally this Thursday, with her foundation for Chloe addressing domestic violence. She has asked me to speak, sharing how Chloe's senseless death has affected my life.'

'That's terrific Sam. Let me know what time and I'll keep you in my thoughts. So, what's your plans for the coming week?'

'Tomorrow, I want to go to the cemetery and spend some time with Chloe and Waru. It will make what's happened so real seeing their headstone and recalling the horror of that week. I will probably feel overwhelmed.'

'When you are there, why don't you call and FaceTime me? I can share your sadness, Sam. Remember, you're never alone. That's what love means, being there for each other. Being united as one means we can share everything.'

'I appreciate that, Letitia. How was I ever so lucky to have had not only one fantastic woman in my life, but now to have a second? I keep thinking, one day I'm going to wake up and find it has been only a dream.'

'Some dream it's been. Especially the last few days before you left. If that was a dream, I don't ever want to wake up,' shared Letitia. 'However, if I do wake up, I'll just keep reliving it and reminding myself how lucky I am.'

'You always know the right thing to say to make a guy feel so good about life. Getting back to what's happening for the rest of the week. Monday I'll catch up with my fellow officers in the CIB at Police Headquarters. I want to see if they have had any success in tracking down the *so-called brother* of Reece Roberts. They found out his name from fingerprint records. Probably mid-week I'll be talking to lawyers for the Prosecution to get an understanding of my part in the trial of Jimmy Johnson. Friday, of course, is Sybil's domestic violence rally. So, my love, it's been a long day. Bed is looking very inviting. I love you beyond the realms of imagination.'

'Likewise, to the moon and back. Sweet dreams, my darling, or maybe I should say, reliving the dream.'

Just as he had discussed with Letitia, the next day Sam spent time with Chloe and Waru, sitting beneath the cooling branches of a nearby tree, reminiscing about special times when he and his wife were happiest. As an air of melancholy cast a veil over his thoughts, he connected with Letitia on FaceTime and immediately felt surrounded by love that brightened up his mood. Peace had returned, as had love. Life never felt more meaningful than it did right at that moment in time.

******

Monday morning, Sam made his way to Police Headquarters to meet up with his fellow detectives in the Criminal Investigation Branch, but he was looking forward mostly to catching up with Detective Sergeant Amos Billings, who was his partner in crime investigations. On seeing Amos, it was like the last nine months evaporated from the past, and time had stood still in that period.

'Great to see you Sammie boy,' was his greeting as they vigorously shook hands. 'Come and sit down and fill me in on what you've been up to since you left to deal with the tragedy of Chloe's death.'

Sam spent the next hour describing all that had happened to him, from his kidnapping in Karumba to his adventure with his mate Blue to the Gemfields, which culminated in the capture of Chloe's killer and finally the circumstances that led to him meeting the new lady in his life, Letitia, and how their friendship had developed into love.

'Bloody hell, Sam. You've had more going on in your life than when you were here covering crime with me. You left out the bit about being tracked by some anonymous whack job who wanted to do you harm. I've heard from Russ Hoffman how you helped take down a career criminal by the name of Reece Roberts and he's got someone here in Bris Vegas who's intent on causing you further retribution. Man, when is it going to end? Seriously though, we're not taking this lightly. We've put out the word on the streets to find out any associates this creep has who could cause you harm.'

'That's some good news, at least, Amos. I'll be glad when this trial next week is over and then the one in Townsville, resulting in a long sentence for the mongrels who violently kidnapped me and left me to die on a deserted island.'

'It doesn't matter how smart these criminals think they are, we have the benefit of science and technology and in the end, they always make a mistake. That's when we'll pounce. Don't lose any sleep Sam, we've got your back. Listen, if you're free after five this afternoon, I'll line up a few of the boys for a beer at the Transcontinental Hotel, down the road.'

'That would be great, Amos. I look forward to it. See you then.'

******

Getting to be in the company of his mates again from the CIB was such a signifying moment for Sam. He felt so embraced to be back in the fold of such a close-knit group. He had shared so much with men and women who had a common goal of achieving justice for innocent victims who, through no fault of their own, had their lives drastically affected by random acts of violence and greed.

There was a nagging thought in the back of his head prompting the question, *was this what he wanted to return to in three months' time*? This had been his chosen career, plus he shared a close fellowship with like-minded people who he knew he could always count on. He had to make some hard decisions as the end of his twelve months of bereavement leave was looming.

What made it so much more difficult was because the previous nine months had been so hectic, he hadn't had the opportunity or time to consider any alternative career options. It was something he needed to discuss with Letitia, considering they had decisions to make about what they wanted from their relationship. He was certain they would have plans for a family in the future that would need to be considered. What else would he be happy doing? Appropriately, being *on the horns of a dilemma* was an apt description of the conflicting emotions he was experiencing.

Chapter Sixteen

Sam was up early, tucking into a breakfast of scrambled eggs, bacon, and strong black coffee, when there was a loud knock on the door. Everybody who knows I'm here, he thought, would have rung to say they were coming. Cautiously, he opened the door to the welcome sight of Senior Sergeant Bob Scott from the Major and Organised Crime Squad, Cloncurry, who had led the raid, which resulted in the capture of Jimmy Johnson.

'Whew, that's a relief, Bob. Come in, great to see you. Have you had breakfast?'

'Great to see you too, mate. Yeah, I had something to eat on the flight from Mt. Isa. I've just come straight from the airport and I found out when I booked in that you were also staying here. What's the story about being cautious and relieved to see me? Has something happened I haven't heard about?'

'Come in and have a coffee and I'll fill you in.' Sam outlined the drama that unfolded with the threatening letter he received in Mt. Isa, followed by circumstances at Carnarvon Gorge, resulting in a Park Ranger being attacked and held captive. While the perpetrator was now in prison, there was the further possibility of a threat in Brisbane from associates of the person responsible for the crime.

'Crikey, no wonder you're skittish. We'll have to be extra vigilant leading up to and during the trial for Chloe's killer. You certainly know how to attract the unwanted attention of certain low life criminal elements.'

'Yeah, and it's making me angry, always looking over my shoulder for threats. Anyway, what's on your agenda leading up to the trial next Monday?'

'Like you, I've got to attend a meeting tomorrow at the office of the Crown Prosecutor. I guess we'll see what eventuates after that. I've also got to check in to Police Headquarters in relation to the trial of Curly Jacobs and Charlie Briggs on the cattle rustling charge and also matters relating to your kidnapping. Other charges of drug dealing have eventuated in response to our ongoing investigations and from questioning of those two drug dealers whose boat you commandeered to escape from that deserted island.'

From his reply, it was clear Sam was experiencing the pressure of continuous built-up tension. 'It seems my last three months of bereavement leave is going to be taken up with attending trials with this one in Brisbane, the one in Townsville, and there will be another for the crimes committed by the perp in Carnarvon Gorge. It's like I haven't stopped working. However, I can't complain. At least my future is brighter because of a relationship that is developing with a wonderful lady I met while trying to track down Jimmy Johnson. We have so much in common, plus both of us share a similar burden, as she had also lost someone tragically.'

'I kind of got a bit of the lowdown from the contact you put us on to, namely Mitchell, who helped us set a trap to capture the cattle rustlers. I remember hearing he had a sister who I believe is the young lady to whom you refer. Congratulations, I couldn't be more happy for you, Sam. Losing Chloe so tragically would be so hard to come back from, so to hear you have found someone to share your burden with, who is also benefiting, must be so revitalising to the spirit of you both.'

'Yes, Letitia is Mitchell's sister. Life or love, whatever you like to call it, certainly moves in mysterious ways. If you don't mind, I'd like to go with you to headquarters to check out what my involvement will be in the Townsville trial. With my leave ending soon, I need to talk to someone about my future as a police officer. I'm not exactly sure whether I want to return to life in Brisbane as a detective, as I fear I'd be haunted by the memory of what happened to Chloe. Her having been a police officer as well would be a constant reminder, regularly encountering people with whom she worked. I'd like to remain in some capacity, but I'm not exactly sure what that looks like or where it might be.'

'We could always use someone with your experience in the MOC squad. Not only do you have the crime fighting capabilities you've developed as a Detective Sergeant but you have a thorough knowledge of all the territory we cover. Your background as a First Nations person from the area would be invaluable also in helping to deal with problems that could be overcome more easily by you having an understanding about sensitive issues relevant to Indigenous affairs. Something for you to think about.'

'That's right out of left field, and something I hadn't contemplated,' replied Sam. 'It would certainly tick a lot of boxes, considering my relationship with Letitia and the path I hope it will take. It certainly makes sense because both of us have family in the area or in close vicinity. Thanks for that idea, Bob. I'll definitely run it past the powers that be at headquarters.'

Sam and Bob spent a large part of the day liaising with various section heads at headquarters in relation to relevant matters. The first was about the future criminal trials at which they were required to give evidence, plus the ongoing threat from unknown persons that could affect Sam's safety. During a chat with Human Resources, Sam put forward the idea of a potential move to the MOC squad based in Cloncurry. They understood the reasons it would better suit him with such a move and assured him they would look at it favourably after talking with both the head of Detectives and also Bob Scott. Sam at least knew the outcome of what the latter discussion would be, which gave him hope to start to think about making plans for his and Letitia's future.

That night, he was excited with his FaceTime conversation with Letitia to inform her of his chat with Bob Scott and the HR department about a likely move to the Gulf region and what that would mean for their future together.

'Oh Sam, that's wonderful news. I haven't thought too seriously about plans for us being together somewhere. I didn't want to jinx where we are at in our relationship now for fear of putting any pressure on you. Now that I know what your thoughts are about us having a more permanent arrangement, it means I can be free to dream.'

'Darling Letitia. A life with you is all that I think about, and what better place to make that happen than somewhere we feel we can belong? That is my traditional country and also close to yours. Feel free to make plans and dream big.' They exchanged many thoughts about what it could all mean until reluctantly Sam had to put further discussions about their future on hold, needing to be well rested for the meeting with Lawyers for the Prosecution next day.

Chapter Seventeen

There were several people already waiting in the office of the Crown Prosecutor, a Mr. Adrian Quartermain. They were Mrs. Joan Cartwright, the concerned neighbour who heard the domestic violence disturbance and called police; Constable Arthur Burns, who had been on the callout and who witnessed the shooting murder of senior Constable Chloe Mackenzie; and Mrs. Noelene Johnson, the wife of the accused, Mr. Jimmy Johnson.

The prosecutor introduced to those already gathered in his office, Senior Sergeant Bob Scott, who led the raid on the property owned by relatives of Jimmy, on suspicion of a suspected large drug operation, and Detective Sergeant Sam Mackenzie, the husband of the murdered woman.

'Thanks for all agreeing to be witnesses for the prosecution. The accused, Mr. Jimmy Johnson, has pleaded not guilty, requiring us to prove he did in fact commit the crime of murder. As this is an informal discussion to determine how the flow of the court case should proceed, the process will flow more smoothly if you are happy that I refer to you by your first names.' Everyone signalled their agreement. 'So, on the evening in question, Joan, you reported to the police a loud disturbance taking place in the house of Jimmy and Noelene Johnson. Tell me why you were so concerned?'

'The Johnson's moved next door about six months before. During that time, I have overheard some loud arguments taking place. This one sounded more violent with banging and crashing. Then I heard children's voices and loud crying, followed by a male voice shouting threats of violence if they didn't shut up. There's been a few cases on the news recently of these domestic violence incidents leading to people being badly injured or even murdered. So, I called triple zero because I was afraid for the family. I feel terrible that Sam's wife Chloe died because she attended the disturbance. I keep asking myself, if I had ignored what was happening, would she still be alive today? I'm so sorry Sam. I don't know how I'll cope when I'm on the witness stand.'

'Don't blame yourself, Joan. That was a reasonable course of action you took that anyone in the same situation would have taken,' offered Sam, as he saw the pain and guilt she was suffering. 'We all know as police officers that having to deal with unstable people has its dangers. You had no way of knowing Jimmy Johnson was going to come out of the house firing a shotgun.'

Adrian agreed with Sam and advised Joan to not be afraid to tell the jury exactly what had occurred, as she had just shared.

Next Adrian addressed Johnson's wife. 'Now, Noelene, would you like to tell us a bit about your relationship with your husband? Had he been violent in the past and what happened on the night in question that led to his threats against you and your children.?'

'I want to say first up I'd met Mrs. Cartwright on quite a few occasions with a few chats over the back fence and I appreciate what she did in ringing the police. I was afraid mostly for the kids that night. Jimmy was often argumentative and domineering and could become violent when he came home drunk and wanting to have sex. Sometimes I resisted him, but it didn't matter. He'd yell out that I was his property and then rape me anyhow. This night he was not only drunk, but I could smell perfume on his clothes. I thought if I accused him of sleeping with other women, he might back off. He went into a rage and started hitting me. That's when the kids came into the bedroom screaming when they saw him punching me.' She started to get emotional and needed a few moments to feel she could continue.

'I don't know how long he ranted and raved for, but next thing I know, someone outside is calling for him to come out peacefully. He had a rifle; I think a shotgun that he would often wave about menacingly, no doubt to create fear in me. He must have grabbed it and headed outside because the next thing I heard was two loud explosions and a short while later, three quick sounds, like bang...bang...bang and a male yelling out, *Police officer down* followed a bit later by sirens and police bursting through the front door. Maybe I should have reported him before that, but his threats and the rifle and the safety of my kids held me back. There was a time I loved him, but he beat that out of me.'

'Thanks Noelene. I'd say yours was a typical case of *battered wife syndrome* where you felt a diminished sense of worth because of the way he treated you and the main thing that enabled you to cope was the need to protect your children. The jury will be completely sympathetic towards your plight, I'm sure. Just be up front with them and retell your story exactly how you just described it.'

The Prosecutor next questioned Constable Burns. 'Arthur, you were with Chloe Mackenzie on that fateful night. Describe what happened when you arrived at the scene.'

'Chloe and I answered the call of a domestic violence incident. When we arrived, we heard a lot of shouting, cursing, and banging noises, like maybe furniture being thrown about. I initially was making my way closer to hear better when Chloe told me to cordon off the house. She had checked for any criminal record for Jimmy Johnson and found he had been charged previously with drug dealing and had been found guilty of illegal gun possession. Chloe requested some backup and called out for Johnson to step outside with his hands raised and to not have any weapons. Next thing I know, someone is running out from beside the house and firing from a shotgun, which unfortunately hit Chloe full force below the bullet-proof vest she wore. Johnson was heading towards some trees as I drew my weapon. I fired three quick shots towards him but he disappeared. I tried to follow, but it was too dark, so I returned to where

Chloe lay wounded and tried to stop the blood flow. I felt so helpless. She was such a wonderful person and I wish it could have been me. I still have nightmares to this day, and the doctors say I'm suffering PTSD. I have just returned to duty recently and want to continue to be a police officer as my way of paying respect for the life of Chloe so tragically lost. Such a wonderful person and friend.'

Adrian Quartermain could see that everyone was suffering various stages of sadness from the three accounts shared, so he called a temporary stay of proceedings. He'd arranged refreshments and something to eat in order to give everyone time to collect their thoughts and refresh before attempting to carry on. An hour later, he reconvened.

'I know the circumstances of a case like this are very harrowing, but unfortunately, the law demands the retelling of what occurred in order to get justice, in this case for a deeply loved and respected member of the police force but also a wife and a mother to be. I can't begin to imagine the grief and pain inflicted on Sam Mackenzie for losing his precious Chloe, but also their unborn son. No doubt Chloe's parents have suffered similar grief and loss. To save you the absolute pain of reliving the aftermath of what happened immediately following news of Chloe's unfortunate wounding and death, perhaps Sam, you can relate the story of how you tracked down Jimmy Johnson.'

'First, I want to thank everyone for their courage in recounting what must have been such a dramatic and terrifying occurrence. I loved Chloe with all my heart and soul, and I have to admit I was in an extremely dark place for a long time. Grief never ends, but it does change. People help and I am thankful for so many for reaching out to give me strength. Someone who I met in Mt. Isa, my hometown where I went to be with family, had heard of a family named Johnson, who had property in central Queensland. I recruited my best mate, Billy *Blue* Williams, to accompany me to the central Queensland Gemfields on the pretence we were fossicking for precious gems. What we were trying to do was get some information about the Johnson's who I'd heard about. To cut a long story short, several unusual occurrences involved a true-blue, dingy-di Aussie bushie, affectionately referred to as *old Bob*. He had a couple of mining leases. One near the Gemfields and another outside Alpha. We learned from his exploits that the Johnson property we wanted to find was close to his Alpha mine. He discovered they were growing marijuana in large quantities when he took a shortcut through their property one day to reach his second mine. That's where Bob Scott comes in. I'd met Bob on another matter involving the rustling of cattle from a property owned by my uncles. Bob can tell you what happened next.'

'Sam rang me to let me know this character, *old Bob,* had accidentally come across this flourishing illegal crop and had even taken the precaution of recording a video and photos, which gave us the proof to get a search warrant for the Johnson property. At this stage, our only intention was discovering the drugs were still on the property and apprehend and arrest those responsible. We had a raiding party to surprise the occupants of the principal residence before they could destroy or hide any evidence or escape. I invited Sam along solely as an observer, but not to take part. However, that was mainly for his safety, as he had suffered enough with the loss of Chloe. He was still a serving police officer, even though he had taken twelve months of bereavement leave to come to terms with his grief. Our tactical officers used stun grenades and smoke devices to flush the occupants out of the house.'

He continued. 'We were in the process of making arrests while Sam was observing at a distance from the safety of a vehicle. Unbeknown to me, there must have been a secret tunnel as a means of escape. Sam saw a stray head pop up from under a tank-stand and a figure take off across the yard, heading for a large shed, which he assumed was where the drugs were stored. Sam started the police vehicle and took chase. The person he wanted to apprehend had a rifle, which he was preparing to fire at the vehicle. Sam took action to avoid being shot by swerving directly at the man. The vehicle hit him with a glancing blow, causing the rifle to fly from his grasp and temporarily knock him to the ground. By the time I got to the scene, Sam had found handcuffs in the cars storage area, which he used to restrain the perpetrator. It wasn't until one of the elderly women we'd apprehended came rushing up using colourful language, claiming we had caused her son Jimmy harm with how he was captured. He had long hair and a big bushy beard, so he was unrecognisable from photos we had of him. To our surprise, we'd captured Chloe's suspected killer. I duly read him his rights and arrested him. The rest is history.'

Pensively, Adrian Quartermain directed a question to Bob Scott, as he had been in charge of the raid on the Johnson property. 'I need to get a definitive statement on an additional matter. There has been an accusation by the defence lawyer for the accused that unnecessary force was used against Jimmy Johnson, specifically mentioning, in their language, *a direct attack by DS Sam Mackenzie*. What can you tell me about that?'

'Sam has already outlined his part in capturing the alleged suspect and what I believe were necessary actions to first protect himself from being shot and secondly to stop the man from escaping. I contend at this point; Sam did not know who the person was. When he learned, it was in fact Jimmy Johnson, the suspected murderer of his wife, I believe he became overwhelmed with anger, fuelled by the grief and the trauma he had been suffering since the death of Chloe. It was also my belief Sam could be experiencing the effects of Post-Traumatic Stress Disorder, which was later confirmed. Sam made a move towards Jimmy Johnson and they came into contact, but not with sufficient force to cause any harm. I intervened before that could happen, for I knew more violence would be detrimental to our future case and because I felt Sam could not control his emotions because of his suffering from the loss of his wife and unborn child.'

'From your account, Bob, I don't believe Johnson's defence can use that to get sympathy from the jury. Thank you all for your forthright evidence. Just relate to the court the account you have all outlined to me today,' indicated Adrian Quartermain. 'I'm as sure as I've ever been with any case I've ever prosecuted; the only verdict can be murder in the first degree of a police officer. Thanks, and I'll see you all next Monday.'

Chapter Eighteen

Sam looked forward to again meeting up with Sybil and Brian, Chloe's parents and taking part in the rally organised to emphasise the importance of addressing the issues of Domestic Violence in the community. He was tentative about going over stressful events from the past that had caused him such grief and pain but knew, in order to make Chloe's death have some long-lasting benefit, he needed to be strong. The event was organised for 12.30pm to take advantage of staff on their lunch break and close to the main Brisbane city precinct for people travelling by public transport.

Approaching midday, the crowd was building quickly at the South Bank Piazza in response to extensive publicity given to the rally by television and radio stations. By the start time, there were hardly any seats available. Queensland police, because of their active role in dealing with domestic violence, had a division which was now directly proactive in efforts to prevent rather than deal with the after-effects of the tragedies they had to attend. A representative from that division was glad to open the rally first by paying respect to the Turrbal First Nations People, on whose land the present-day city of Brisbane stood and to all Traditional Owners, their Elders, past, present and emerging. She next welcomed Sybil to speak about her experience of domestic violence with the loss of her daughter.

'Thank you all for attending our rally. It shows how so many in the community feel about this subject, which in recent times has become so prevalent. As many of you may be aware, I lost my beautiful daughter, Chloe, because of a domestic violence situation she was attending in her role as a police officer. I also lost my unborn grandson, who Chloe was pregnant with when she was killed. I keep asking myself, why are there so many domestic violence incidents in the first place? The answer I come up with always is RESPECT. Respect for the rights especially of women but respect of everyone's rights. I know when I was growing up, my parents were most emphatic about teaching us to respect others. So that therefore is a societal problem and some aspects of society as we once knew it have broken down, one of those being the family unit. People are not learning those values in the home anymore. So how do we now instil in the young ones growing up the values which we hope will become the cornerstone of society in the future? The answer undoubtedly starts with the education of our young, which must now take place in the schools, as the home doesn't seem to be where that happens anymore. I now ask my husband Brian to talk to you about the devastation caused by domestic violence, speaking from our experience.' There was a standing ovation for Sybil as she handed over to Brian.

'Thanks for that overwhelming affirmation for Sybil. I'm sure that gives her strength because I can tell you what Sybil has endured, the grief and utter hopelessness she has gone through, as the woman who bore Chloe, imparting her love and respect for others. It's something you wouldn't want your worst enemy to experience. So that is my first message to you all today.' Brian continued to explain further.

'I, like Sybil, have suffered the grief and pain of losing someone you've brought into this world and watched grow up to be a caring and loving individual, full of the hopes and dreams that no doubt all of you out there today have. But it's also the wives and children involved in the many incidents occurring, who have their lives irreparably changed. I know there are people out there who have a violent nature or are controlling in different ways. I think being proactive, as the police are these days, helps to identify problems which are occurring and take immediate action to prevent them from becoming statistics. Different organisations have been for a long-time helping women and families to escape homes where violence is happening by providing safe houses. Governments also have to be more involved, especially in providing financial support but also the backing of health professionals like psychiatrists and experts in trauma management. We've decided our initiative will be to approach media outlets to regularly circulate the places where those in vulnerable situations can get help, like St. Vincent De Paul and Lifeline. I recommend these things to you today and ask you to welcome Sam Mackenzie, the husband of our beloved Chloe, to the stage.' Again, the audience showed their appreciation for Brian with loud applause.

'Hi, you're such an appreciative audience, the way you've shown your support for Sybil and Brian. As they have mentioned, the emotional toll because of domestic violence cannot be emphasised enough. It is now nine months since I lost my beautiful Chloe and our unborn son, who we would have named Waru, which in the language of the Kalkadoon people from whom I descend means *the Milky Way*. Whenever I am seeking comfort because of their loss, I go outside, look up at the night skies and believe they are looking down on me and I feel they are still there showering their love on me. That has been one way I have been able to cope with the grief of losing them. The wishes of good friends and having people around me who have cared and reached out with their love and kindness are also paramount. I am a police officer, as Chloe was, and we know only too well the toll domestic violence takes on so many lives. The perpetrators of these criminal acts, if they are prosecuted, have their liberty taken away in the form of a jail sentence that disrupts their lives for a short number of years. The real toll is those they have caused harm to, who suffer a life sentence. Grief never ends. But it changes. It's purely a place in time, but not a place to remain. It's neither a sign of weakness, nor is it a lack of faith. It is the price of love. I believe love will always prevail, overcoming hatred and evil. Go in love, my friends, and if I can ask one thing, would you turn to the person next to you and extend a hand of friendship? I would also ask you to support Sybil and Brian with their foundation in memory of Chloe and the victims of domestic violence.'

That evening, on all the Brisbane news channels, footage was shown of the packed South Bank Piazza and the ending scene of about half the audience shaking hands but more surprisingly to the newsreaders and no doubt to people tuning in, a good percentage of the other half were embracing each other.

'Could this be a seminal moment in taking a more positive and precise stand against domestic violence?' were Sam's sentiments upon viewing this outpouring of love and friendship.

That evening, Sam was delighted to relate to Letitia the outcome of the meeting with the Crown Prosecutor and the successful rally in the name of Chloe for the fight against domestic violence. 'Oh Sam, I'm so proud of you for the powerful message you could share, and also Chloe's parents. Out of tragedy comes hope. I love you so much. I can't wait for you to return.'

Chapter Nineteen

It was Friday morning, and Sam was free for the next three days. He was wondering how he might fill his time in when his phone pinged. He was alarmed by the message he received.

You can't help yourself, can you copper? I wondered what happened to you after the capture of one of our brotherhood in Carnarvon. There on the news last night, you bobbed up speaking at a rally. You must like these rallies where you first came on our radar. Now I'm on your trail. Not only you. How about your do-gooder ex In-laws? You can run, but you can't hide. I'll be seeing ya' copper.

He immediately rang Bob Scott to advise him of the disturbing message he had just received. Bob was soon knocking on Sam's door. 'First thing is we alert our mates at Police Headquarters. The message mentions Chloe's parents, so how about you ring them straight away so they can take steps to keep safe?

Sybil answered with sounds of heavy breathing. 'Are you alright Sybil? You sound stressed.'

'I'm fine Sam, I'm out walking with Brian and we have just climbed a steep hill, hence the breathlessness. How can we help?'

'I don't want you to be alarmed Sybil, but I've just received a threatening text message following our appearance at the domestic violence rally. I hadn't told you about some threats via text messages I received previously, as I didn't think it relevant or saw any need to worry you. I didn't think there'd be any more messages after we captured the originator of the earlier messages. It now appears he has been in cahoots with someone here in Brisbane who is carrying on this vendetta against me. In this latest text, he also mentions *my Ex In-Laws*. That's why I'm ringing so you can be on your guard. I don't know if it has anything to do with the court case starting Monday, but we're contacting the local police to investigate.'

'It seems to me, Sam, that we should all get out of town until the trial starts. If you're not doing anything, how about we all head down to the Gold Coast where Brian and I have a holiday house we share with the family?'

'That sounds great, Sybil. I am here with Senior Sergeant Bob Scott, who is down from Cloncurry. He led the raid that captured Jimmy Johnson, so he is also giving evidence for the prosecution next week. Do you mind him coming along? We are good friends.'

'No worries. Any friend of yours is a friend of ours. It's now 8.00am. Where and when shall we pick you up?'

'We're going to headquarters now to put the threat into the hands of the police experts. When you are getting close, call me and we'll be waiting outside

Police Headquarters, Roma Street, say about 11.00am. We should be safe enough there.'

At the agreed time, Sam and Bob joined Sybil and Brian for the escape to the Gold Coast. 'This is better than being locked up in your apartment wondering who might be lurking around the place. We'll even get to do some tourist type things,' commented Brian. 'It's currently whale migration season where they travel up from Antarctica to the warmer waters of North Queensland to find a mate and do what comes naturally, so to speak.'

'I think we can read between the lines, Brian. It's something I've always wanted to do,' advised Bob, 'but living in the outback, the only marine life that until now excites me, has been catching a barramundi.'

'Perhaps we can trade experiences, Bob. I've always wanted to try my hand at catching a big barra.'

'Any time Brian. Just let me know when you're heading to the outback and we'll organise a trip to the Gulf. Perhaps by then Sam might be enjoying a lifestyle change and join us.'

'Hello?' queried Sybil. 'Please explain. What's that all about?'

'Bob and I have been discussing a career change with me working for him in Cloncurry,' Sam explained. 'Since spending bereavement leave with family in Mt. Isa, I've been thinking I'd like to live closer to them. I also have my roots with the Kalkadoon First Nations people whose culture I want to find out more about from the elders and learn about the Dreaming stories of my ancestors. I feel I've lost touch with it since I've lived in Brisbane after going to university here and then joining the police. It's early days yet. Maybe, as Brian says, you can spend more time in my country in the future.'

'We'd love that, Sam,' confirmed Sybil. 'We're happy you can feel closer to your culture and your family. We are your family too and will always want to be in your life. It will give us an excuse to see more of North Queensland.'

The weekend turned out to be a wonderful time of sharing and enjoying different unique experiences, including a whale watching trip, a visit to Movie World, and the Australian Outback Spectacular's Heartland show and dinner, which gave a representation of outback life, especially valuable for people in the mainland cities. While Sam and Bob both agreed they couldn't pick their favourite, they both agreed the friendship of Sybil and Brian was what stood out for them. It was made special by their kindness and generosity and getting them into a headspace to approach Monday's trial in a relaxed frame of mind. They were on the road before daybreak Monday morning to be in Brisbane in plenty of time to get ready for the court case. Sybil and Brian had bought clothes with them which they could change into at Sam's apartment, to be on hand at the trial to finally achieve justice for their murdered daughter, Chloe.

Chapter Twenty

Most of the first morning was taken up with jury selection prior to the trial, starting after lunch. The prosecutor, Adrian Quartermain, spent the rest of the day introducing into proceedings several of his witnesses who tendered their testimony as they had rehearsed it in Adrian's office previously. The defence lawyers appearing for the accused, Jimmy Johnson, queried some statements and objected to how certain questions by the prosecutor were framed, however, there was little chance to score points in favour of their client. Proceedings concluded on the first day with the testimonies of Senior Sergeant Bob Scott and Detective Sergeant Sam Mackenzie to still be heard.

Present in the courtroom for the entire day was Sam's detective partner, Amos Billings. He was on hand, accompanied by two uniformed police officers, to escort Sam and Bob safely back to their apartment. 'We can't have you getting attacked on the street before you put that grub Johnson away for life,' remarked Amos. 'Unfortunately, we haven't been able to track down the source of the phone threats, so we're taking every precaution necessary in the meantime. We'll also have an officer placed in the corridor outside your rooms until the trial is over.'

Amos was invited to join Bob and Sam in his apartment for a quiet drink and chat about the possible connection between the author of the latest phone threats and the original ones from the criminal that had been captured over the Carnarvon Gorge incident.

'In the latest text, reference is made to *the brotherhood*, whereas in the first text, he used the term *one of our brothers*. Is there a clue in the use of a different term? Maybe they are trying to confuse us on purpose.'

'As I advised you the other day, your perp Reece Roberts has a brother, however we have ruled him out. The term *the brotherhood* is fairly common with criminal organisations like Bikie gangs. We'll keep checking any connections that might relate to such groups.'

******

The trial resumed Tuesday morning, with Bob Scott first to testify. He began by explaining they'd raided the Johnson property, located close to the town of Alpha, following the issuing of a warrant on suspicion of illegal drugs being grown. He outlined the following. 'The capture of Jimmy Johnson was purely the result of him being on the property at the time. We did not know of him being present beforehand and he was not the purpose of the raid.'

The defence queried what evidence was used to enable a warrant to be issued in the first place. Bob advised that, 'a local prospector who had a mine on land next to the Johnson's place had cut through the Johnson property as a shortcut and discovered a healthy crop of marijuana. He took photos and a video which were referred to me to take the appropriate action.'

The defence asked the judge to order the photos and video to be ruled as inadmissible, as it was their belief the miner who took the photos and video had illegally trespassed. The judge took the view the miner had innocently come across evidence of what he believed was an illegal activity, not because of any prior suspicion that drugs were being grown, but because he tried to get easier access to his mine. It was the judge's opinion that the miner had a duty to report evidence of criminal activity. Anyhow, he believed it had no relevance in the apprehending of Jimmy Johnson and dismissed the request.

Next up was Detective Sergeant Sam Mackenzie. Sam advised he had been asked to accompany Senior Sergeant Bob Scott on the raid, as he was a friend of the miner who had obtained the evidence of an illegal crop. 'I had befriended the miner referred to during a trip to the Gemfields in central Queensland. After my wife Chloe had been fatally shot, I needed to take bereavement leave to deal with my grief and try to find a reason to go on living again. The miner who asked me to refer to him as *old Bob* was sympathetic to my situation and also knew I was a police officer. He gave me the evidence he had accidentally come across. I, in turn, gave Bob Scott the photos and video for whatever action he deemed necessary. That's the reason I was invited to accompany Bob on the raid, but only as an observer, not a participant. As Senior Sergeant Bob Scott and his team were involved with occupants in the main house, I observed a person who could be involved in the growing of an illegal drug escaping, via a tunnel, and I had no alternative but to apprehend the person. I took whatever means necessary, especially when I was threatened by a rifle being aimed at me.'

'So,' the defence lawyer queried, 'you did not use unnecessary force to waylay the escaping person?'

'That's correct,' confirmed Sam. 'I believe my safety was being threatened by the possibility of being shot.'

'So, when you had the prisoner restrained, is it not true that you attempted to attack him again?' accused the defence lawyer.

'When one woman, under the arrest of officer Scott, called me a rotten scoundrel, plus a few other expletives, for what I had done to her poor Jimmy, I realised that the person I had detained was in fact Jimmy Johnson. He had long hair and a big bushy beard, so he looked different from photos I had seen. He was the accused killer of my wife Chloe, the love of my life. I guess in that moment of recognition and faced with the reality her suspected murderer was there in front of me, I lost it. I lunged at him in anger. Thankfully, Bob Scott grabbed me before I could cause the prisoner any harm.'

'Is that what happened, officer Scott?' asked the Judge.

'Yes, your honour. Sam Mackenzie's state at that moment I would describe as one of uncontrollable emotion as he broke down and burst into tears after

I intervened. I don't believe it was a matter of him seeking revenge so much as the outpouring of a build-up of months of grief he had been dealing with following his wife Chloe's death.'

The Judge addressed the defence lawyer on his opinion. 'Considering Officer Mackenzie had unknowingly captured the person who he believed was the killer of his wife, I would say under the circumstances, his actions were involuntary and spur of the moment, because of the grief he no doubt had been suffering ever since her death. I don't see any purpose in the defence pursuing that line of questioning any further. Do you have anything additional to add?'

'No, your honour.'

'Then I direct the defence to make your closing statement and following that the prosecution will sum up their case.'

At the completion of the summaries by both parties, the judge directed the jury to adjourn to come to an agreement as to the innocence or guilt of the accused. However, as it was almost time to finish for the day, he retired the jury and advised them to return fresh Wednesday morning to take whatever time they required to make their decision and then report back to the Court their verdict.

Detective Sergeant Billings and two police constables accompanying him acted as escorts for Sam Mackenzie and Bob Scott to return them safely to their accommodation.

'There's probably no sense in escorting you to the courthouse tomorrow until the jury makes their decision. I will be alerted when they are ready to hand down their verdict and I will be back to accompany you to the court. I don't reckon they will take too long. I think it is a slam-dunk. So, I'll see you early,' said Amos.

Chapter Twenty-One

Detective Billings picked Sam and Bob up at 11.00am Wednesday as the jury were ready to hand down their verdict. They were sitting in the court, ready and waiting thirty minutes later.

The judge addressed the jury, asking the foreperson if they had agreed on a verdict.

'Yes, your honour,' she replied.

'What is your verdict in the case of the Crown versus Mr. Jimmy Johnson on the charge of first-degree murder of a police officer?'

'The jury finds Mr. Jimmy Johnson guilty as per the charges of first-degree murder of police officer Chloe Mackenzie, you honour.'

The judge discharged the jury, allowing them to leave the court.

The judge then asked the accused Mr. Jimmy Johnson to stand.

'Mr. Johnson. You have been found guilty of murder in the first degree of Senior Constable Chloe Mackenzie. For the murder of a police officer, I sentence you to the maximum term of 25 years. Please escort the prisoner from this court.'

Sam and Bob quickly found Chloe's parents, Sybil and Brian, to join them in an emotionally charged group hug. 'Justice at last for Chloe and our unborn son, Waru,' rejoiced Sam, with tears in his eyes. 'This calls for a celebration. How about we head to the Transcontinental Hotel?'

With their escort of Detective Amos Billings and the two constables, they headed down George Street towards the hotel. They came to the lights on Herschel Street, close to the hotel, waiting for traffic lights to change before crossing. Sam and Chloe's parents were standing right on the edge with the others several metres behind when someone flashed out of nowhere, pushing Sam into a lane of traffic that was just speeding up over the crossing. Sam slammed into the side of an advancing vehicle and was thrown back onto the footpath, heavily falling unconscious onto the hard concrete. Bob Scott raced to Sam to check on his condition while Amos and the constables took off in pursuit of Sam's attacker. He'd headed up Herschel Street and across Roma Street, racing towards the Roma Street Parkland.

Amos immediately contacted headquarters for backup, advising them of the situation while the constables continued the pursuit. The Parkland was a fairly contained area and Amos needed the backup to close off any points of escape while also requesting a police dog to flush out their suspect should he seek to hide amongst any foliage that in some places was dense. As he caught up with the constables, he could hear the sirens as police vehicles sped to surround the Parklands.

Meanwhile, back at the scene of the attack, an ambulance had arrived with paramedics to tend to Sam. They checked his vital signs prior to taking urgent action to get him to a hospital to fully assess his condition. Sybil was inconsolable as Bob, along with her husband Brian, tried to ease her pain of seeing Sam suffering such injury. As the ambulance was pulling away with lights and sirens, Bob flagged down a taxi and was able to get the driver to follow the vehicle carrying Sam. The paramedics rushed Sam into the Emergency and Trauma Centre at the Royal Brisbane and Women's Hospital, so medical staff could determine the extent of Sam's injuries.

******

The situation at the Roma Street Parkland had become a full-on search of any place where Sam's attacker might hide. A recently acquired EC-135 helicopter was also dispatched to give a better view of the area and to keep an aerial eye on the suspect should he escape from the Parkland area. This proved a masterstroke as a man emerged from behind some trees close to Wickham Terrace, having evaded the Parkland searchers and headed towards the city centre. Police from the Parkland were alerted, and along with their attack dogs, were quickly in pursuit, assisted by advice from the helicopter crew.

Fortunately, other police officers on duty in the city headed toward Wickham Terrace, and soon the fleeing suspect was surrounded. When he saw his plight, he grabbed the nearest person, which happened to be a young fashionably dressed woman. He had his arm firmly around her neck while threatening to inflict injury with a knife. Police advised him to release the girl and drop the knife. The attack dogs were still on their leashes, awaiting their opportunity to charge. The suspect was wearing sneakers, which meant when the young girl stomped down heavily with her stiletto healed shoe on his right foot, he yelped in pain, letting her go. The attack dogs were released, one grabbing the arm holding the knife, the other taking hold of the man's leg as he screamed loudly from the gnashing teeth which sank deeply into his flesh. He was thumped heavily to the ground, handcuffed, and eventually led to an enclosed wagon to be processed back at headquarters.

******

Chloe's mother and father were grief stricken, casting their minds back to a similar situation some nine months prior when they awaited the medical diagnoses of injuries suffered by their daughter. It was beyond belief that Sam was now suffering a similar fate. After over an hour of waiting, a doctor emerged, ushering them into a nearby office to outline the extent of Sam's injuries.

'We have tended to Sam's visible injuries, which were composed of bleeding from a knock to his head and also an injured right arm, which we have tended to and is not considered a serious issue. We have taken head scans and there is also some bleeding on the brain. For that reason, we have put him into an induced coma. Please don't be alarmed. This is usual practice in cases like this. The purpose is to allow healing to happen and for swelling to reduce. We will then be able to work on Sam's recovery. We won't know until the swelling goes down how Sam will be affected, but we are hopeful for a positive outcome. It will be a few days before we know anything definitive. There's nothing you can do by staying at the hospital. When we start to see an improvement, I will ring you and you can spend some time with him then. Sam's vital signs are good, so keep your hopes strong.'

'Thanks doctor. Do you mind if we visit him briefly,' asked Sybil, 'just in case he can sense our presence and feel comforted? He has a young lady up in Central Queensland who will be distraught about the news of Sam's injuries. I'm sure she will be a bit more relieved to know we've seen him.'

'Yes, by all means, talk to him. Hearing a familiar voice may be some comfort to him. It could be a good stimulation for his brain. I'll be in touch and don't worry. We have the best head trauma specialists in the business. He's in excellent hands.'

Sybil was dreading the next duty of ringing Letitia and informing her of Sam's injuries. When she arrived home with Brian, she broke down when she walked into the house and saw a photo of Chloe and Sam at their wedding.

'Don't worry, love,' advised Brian, 'you're in no state to talk to Letitia. I'll break it to her as gently as I can.'

There was no easy way of breaking the terrible news, for however he did it, he knew she would be an emotional mess. He explained how they were present when Sam was attacked and were able to see him in hospital. He described how Sam was placed in an induced coma, which was a normal practice with head trauma patients, and not to worry because he was in the capable hands of the best medical professionals. As expected, Letitia was heartbroken and inconsolable, but appreciative of the fact he was in good care.

'Oh my God, Brian,' her words sounding choked with sorrow, 'that's the worst news possible. Are you and Sybil, okay? I can't imagine how you are feeling, having seen it happen and also remembering what you went through when Chloe was fatally injured. I must catch a flight to Brisbane to be with my darling Sam. I'll ring Sam's friend Russell Hoffman in Emerald to get me on the next available flight.'

'The doctor said it could be several days before he shows improvement, so don't stress if you can't get away immediately. As soon as you know when you'll arrive, let me know and we'll meet you at the airport. Try to get some rest and try not to worry, although I know that will be near to impossible. Do you have someone with whom you can share your sorrow? You'll need their comfort and strength.'

'Yes, my parents are here, also my brother Mitchell. He has formed a close friendship with Sam as well. He might even want to travel with me to Brisbane.'

'That's wonderful that you have someone close. If Mitchell does travel with you, Sybil and I will be happy for you both to stay with us.'

'Thanks for calling, Brian, and for your generous offer to stay with you. I'll talk to you soon. Take care of Sybil. I know it will be a difficult time for you both, but I know you'll be a great support and comfort for Sam and me, too.'

Chapter Twenty-Two

The first thing Detective Sergeant Amos Billings did when he had returned to headquarters with Sam Mackenzie's attacker was to process him and take his fingerprints and DNA. He then ran the fingerprints through the police system and came up with a match for a previous offender by the name of Jessie Cameron. He had a criminal record for several offences, the main ones being for drug trafficking; break and enter; stealing motor vehicles and robbery with violence. After informing Jessie Cameron of his rights, Amos charged him with the violent attack of a police officer; escaping the scene of a crime; taking as a hostage, a member of the public; threat with a deadly weapon and resisting arrest.

In the company of his current detective partner, Amos set up an interview with Sam Mackenzie's attacker. 'The time is 10.30am. Present are DS Amos Billings, and DS Arnold Thompson, interviewing suspect Jessie Cameron for his alleged attack on DS Sam Mackenzie. The interview is being recorded. Mr. Cameron, we know your name and we're aware of your association with a suspect by the name of Reece Roberts, charged with several offences in Central Queensland. We are under the understanding you both belong to some type of brotherhood or gang. Together, you seem intent on bringing harm to DS Mackenzie. What is your reason for this vendetta and how does it relate to this brotherhood or gang you belong to?'

'Do you think I'm stupid copper? I'm not about to make your job easier. Figure it out yourself. All I'll say is we're like that serpent in Greek mythology, the Hydra. We have several heads. Cut one off and another one pops up. You think you can stop us? You're in for a surprise.'

'One thing we're sure of is that no matter how many heads there are, we've had no trouble lopping the first two off. You haven't proven too smart so far. I think we're wasting our time here, Arnold. Interview suspended at 10.53am. We'll see if we can track down that multi-headed snake our perp has referred to and lop off all its heads.'

******

Letitia had contacted Russell Hoffman in Emerald, who arranged two seats for a flight to Brisbane on Friday at 3.30pm. Escorting Letitia and Mitchell to the Emerald airport, Russ expressed his sympathy for what had happened to Sam. 'I don't know what to say Letitia. I've known Sam ever since we joined up together. What has happened now, on top of what he has gone through in the last nine months, after losing Chloe, it is so unfair for the truly top person he is. My thoughts and best wishes are with you. Please keep me informed of his condition and hopefully positive progress.'

'Thanks Russell. It's heartening to know so many people care so much for Sam. If that counts for anything in helping him fight back from this, then I'm sure he'll be doing his best to recover.'

On their arrival at Brisbane airport, Sybil and Brian were waiting to welcome them. Letitia introduced them to her brother, Mitchell. The first request Letitia had was to go to the hospital to see Sam, which they obliged by heading directly there. Entering the intensive care unit, they found Sam hooked up to an array of monitors, with tubes protruding from several parts of his body. Although Letitia was overcome with grief and feeling desolate and bereft, she was conscious of not showing sadness or negative emotions. She lovingly reached out and held Sam's hands, at the same time leaning over to kiss his cheeks.

'My darling Sam, I love you so much. I want you to know I am here and we're going to get through this together. I've been in touch with your best mate, Bluey Williams, and his fiancée, Aimee. They send you their love and best wishes for a speedy recovery, and your close friend, Russell Hoffman, does as well. Blue Williams has also let your parents know. You've got so much love coming your way that you'll be back with us in no time.'

Letitia wanted to sit with Sam while Sybil, Brian and Mitchell went to track down a doctor to find out the latest on Sam's condition and hopeful recovery. When they located him, he had some positive news. 'Sam is responding well to treatment. His most recent head scan showed a slight decrease in the swelling of his brain. We will do another scan Monday morning and if things keep progressing like they have, I intend to bring him out of his induced coma. Then it will be a matter of keeping him stable while he continues to heal. At this stage, we don't think he has suffered damage that can't be reversed; however, he has a couple of weeks of intensive care. I'm sure he will also be surrounded by his loving friends and family, which is also important during the healing process. After he comes out of the coma, he should be conscious and able to talk, although he probably won't remember what happened to him. In the meantime, you can visit and sit with him. It's important not to tire him out by staying too long. Rest is the most important part of his recovery. Just increase your visit a bit more each day.'

'Thanks, doctor, for the wonderful care you are taking of Sam,' said Sybil. 'We'll be guided by your advice. I think we're all relieved by the positive outlook you have for Sam's recovery. We'll relay that to his fiancée, Letitia, who is with him at the moment. It will be like a ray of sunshine to her soul.'

When Sybil informed Letitia of the doctor's comments, she broke down in tears, however they were tears of joy and hope and love.

Chapter Twenty-Three

Senior Sergeant Bob Scott needed to return to the MOC squad station in Cloncurry. Before catching his flight, he checked in to Police Headquarters to get the latest from DS Amos Billings concerning Sam Mackenzie's assailant, Jessie Cameron and what his connection was to Reece Roberts, the perpetrator of the kidnapping offence in the Carnarvon Gorge, which was supposed to serve as a threat to Sam Mackenzie.

'I was thinking overnight about those two characters,' indicated Bob. 'It crossed my mind about two plausible scenarios. From what I believe is the case, both these guys have served time for drug dealing. Flowing on from that, I was wondering whether maybe they were in prison at the same time. Could they have struck up a criminal partnership from there? If, as Cameron claims, they are like a multi-headed snake, there could be others serving a similar sentence at the same time who have also become part of their drug dealing syndicate. You remember, Sam was assaulted in Karumba, kidnapped and left to die on a deserted island. It has been confirmed that a guy by the name of Curly Jacobs and his accomplice, Charlie Briggs, were responsible. These two career criminals were involved in drug smuggling activities using ships plying their trade in the Gulf of Carpentaria. Sam Mackenzie is scheduled to give evidence at their trial in Townsville three weeks from next Monday, depending on how he recovers from this latest attack on him. Another person who has agreed to give evidence against Jacobs and Briggs is a guy named Bernie McInerney who with his partner had a boat full of drugs that happened to be the one Sam captured and used to escape from the island where he'd been abandoned. The common denominator in all the characters I've outlined is they have a background in drug dealing. It could be a coincidence, but I don't believe in coincidences. What if the multi-headed snake has an entire network of criminals we need to identify? Is there still danger from others we don't know about? Are you doing anything to ensure Sam is kept safe to enable him to give evidence at the Townsville trial?'

'Interesting idea, Bob, and it is a line of inquiry worth following up on. We'll check criminal records around the time Jessie Cameron and Reece Roberts were in prison to see if there's any connection with other known drug dealers. The Drug Squad also have undercover officers who we'll alert to the possibility. They can ferret out leaks circulating in the criminal world of close associates of those two perpetrators. We'll also source information from our undercover officers. We'll need to keep Sam Mackenzie safe so he can testify in the Townsville trial. Leave it with us, Bob. We'll be in touch and don't worry about Sam. He has a special place in all our hearts with what he has had to endure. His safety is our priority. They won't get a second chance.'

******

Letitia visited Sam in intensive care over the next three days, waiting anxiously for Monday when she hoped and prayed, he would emerge from his induced coma, able to communicate and show signs his health setbacks were only temporary. She was pleased with the police's presence to ensure his ongoing safety. While she sat with Sam, she held his hands and relayed the heartfelt expressions of love and best wishes for a full recovery that came pouring in from so many friends and associates. She talked about the wonderful times they had spent together since their first meeting at Rubyvale, and of her hopes and dreams for their future. If love was the elixir of life, then his path back to full health was paved with bright promise.

Monday arrived, finding Letitia in a state of uneasiness, prancing around Sybil and Brian's home, waiting for the phone call from Sam's specialist to inform them of his condition after he was brought out of his induced coma. Letitia's brother Mitchell was her strength through the anxious wait, calming her down and giving her positive affirmations to not let her emotions spiral out of control. When the phone rang after midday, Mitchell grabbed hold of it first. As a smile spread across his face, Letitia broke down in tears, hugging her brother and grasping the phone almost breathlessly, asking the question, 'is my beautiful Sam going to be, okay?'

'Yes, my dear. His scans were great, and he is now conscious and sitting up. We have a couple more tests to carry out, but you can have a quick word with him first, then after 3.00pm he can have visitors. Thankfully, he has a robust constitution which has held him in good stead. Here's Sam now,'

'Hello, my darling Letitia. Thanks for being with me while I was unconscious. I'm sure your presence helped give me the willpower to come back quickly. Everything's like a hazy fog at the moment, but the doctor said I should start to remember some of what happened with the help of those present when I was attacked. How are you? I hope I didn't give you too much of a scare. I've got to stop making myself a target. I think I want a quieter life and just enjoy being with you. All I want is to love you.'

'That's on the top of my bucket list too, Sam. I'll let you go now so you can get the extra tests the doctor mentioned. I'll be there to see you after three this afternoon. It's at times like this that I know how much I love you and how much I want to spend the rest of my life just loving you. A safer life would be nice, too. See you soon.'

Sam was showered with love not only from Letitia but also Sybil and Brian; his mates in the police force, Amos Billings, Bob Scott and Russell Hoffman; but especially his best mate, Bluey Williams, and his partner, Aimee. Letitia's parents and *old Bob,* his miner mate, had also contacted him excited about Bailey and Riley soon having a litter of pups. 'I'll save the best of the litter for you, my good friend,' he assured Sam. 'There's nothing like a devoted dog to help you feel better. Not forgetting your lovely lady friend, Letitia, who I'm sure is showering you with love.'

Chapter Twenty-Four

Sam's recovery was very rapid with the great level of care from the Royal Brisbane and Women's Hospital staff and the rehabilitation program he was immediately placed into. His detective partner when he was an active officer, DS Amos Billings, visited to check on his progress first-up and to expand on the ideas put forward by Senior Sergeant Bob Scott before he departed Brisbane.

'Great to see you looking so good, mate. I've got to apologise that we weren't able to protect you from the attack which put you in your current state. He came out of nowhere and pushed you into moving traffic and bolted before we could even react. We chased him and cornered him when he tried to use a young woman as a hostage. She had the presence of mind to ram her stiletto heel into his foot. The police dogs charged in and caused him damage when they sank their teeth in and dragged him down. We've found out the bloke's named Jessie Cameron, a career criminal, previously having spent time in prison. Thanks to an idea Bob Scott had, we've delved deeper into his prison term and found out a whole slew of fellow criminals, also serving time for drug dealing who we are looking at more closely. One of those was that Reece Robson who you apprehended in Carnarvon Gorge when he made threats against you and kidnapped one of the park Rangers.'

'Glad to hear you caught the mongrel. I can tell you I'm getting sick of being a target. It started when I got king-hit in Karumba and then left for dead on a deserted island. That all happened after I posed as a drug dealer hoping to find out intel about some people involved in cattle rustling from my uncle's cattle station, but also suspected of supplying drugs to local dealers.'

'That's the angle we're now working on with the Drug Squad after we followed up on Bob Scott's proposition that the association formed between Jessie Cameron and Reece Robson could have wider involvement with drug dealers present in the prison system when they were all behind bars. We think there could be more than the two we know of who form part of a wider organisation. Hence the reference by Jessie Cameron to a snake with multiple heads. Lop one off and another one pops up. We're working on the premise there could be a state-wide operation all connected somehow with what you found out in Karumba. That being the case, when you get discharged, if you're fit enough to travel, you'll have to go into witness protection until your court appearance in Townsville.'

'That certainly makes me feel a lot happier. Do you think that protection can be extended to Letitia? She was the initial target of their threat in Carnarvon, but as I was her bodyguard, Reece Roberts then chose another Ranger to abduct as a warning of his intentions. I'd be a lot less stressed also if I knew Letitia wasn't going to be a target.'

'I don't think there'd be a problem with that, but I'll ring headquarters straight away to get a confirmation,' advised Amos. Five minutes later, he had a decision about allowing Letitia to be under the same protection as Sam.

'I'm sure Letitia will be as pleased as I am with that decision. I think by the end of this week or early next week at the latest, I will get the all-clear to leave the hospital. They don't like to keep you in any longer than necessary, plus I'm not that keen on hospitals, except in extreme times of need.'

'Okay, I'll head back to the station and put the wheels in motion to be ready when you get out,' advised Amos.

Sam immediately rang Letitia so she could contact her boss at the Carnarvon Gorge to advise him she could go into witness protection, for her own safety, at least until after the Townsville trial set down for just over two weeks hence.

Letitia rang back an hour later. 'Hi darling. My boss in charge of Carnarvon Gorge Rangers approves the opportunity for me to stay with you. It's wonderful we can be together, me being your nurse during your recovery, like you were my bodyguard when I needed your protection.'

In between his rehabilitation sessions, Sam became proactive in getting all the information he needed to be prepared for the upcoming trial. He kept in touch by phone and by the use of FaceTime to chat with Bob Scott of the MOC squad but also Senior Sergeant Mick Jenkins from the Karumba police. He'd worked with Mick when they had interviewed the two drug dealers whose boat it was that Sam had commandeered to escape from his island prison. He told Mick what had happened with the trial of Jimmy Johnson and the subsequent attack on him and hospitalisation occurring immediately after.

'It's great to speak to you again, Mick. What a bugger of a couple of weeks I've been through. No doubt you'll be at the trial in Townsville to give evidence. One lead my mates in the CIB are following is that the drug activities we uncovered in the Gulf of Carpentaria could be part of a larger operation with criminals in other areas of Queensland. Perhaps you can see what you can find out from your end.' Mick said he'd check into it and let Sam know.

'Yes, a matter that started out as something we thought was just a local issue in the Gulf of Carpentaria appears it could be much bigger. I might get my Townsville police connection to interview Bernie McInerney again, as he has agreed to give evidence involving the activities of Curly Jacobs and Charlie Briggs. He might have heard something in prison awaiting the trial. I'll let you know the outcome. All the best for a rapid recovery.'

Chapter Twenty-Five

Sam's injuries continued to heal and with less than two weeks before the scheduled trial in Townsville of Curly Jacobs and Charlie Briggs, the doctors gave Sam the clearance to leave hospital. However, he was under strict instructions to not put himself into any situations where he could incur further head injury as his brain would be susceptible to irreparable damage.

Detective Sergeant Amos Billings was on hand to escort Sam and Letitia to their safe house so he could continue towards fully recovery. He made sure there was no chance that any criminal elements would find out their location.

'You can both have peace of mind that you are safe, so there is no pressure or stress to interrupt your healing,' Amos assured them. 'Now, in relation to what will happen regarding getting you safely to Townsville. The Friday prior to the trial, we will escort you to where POLAIR are based for a flight aboard one of their jets. Then in Townsville, you will be under constant surveillance to ensure your safety. There have been developments from our investigations into links between different criminals who were in prison for drug dealing at the same time as Jessie Cameron and Reece Robson. There are an additional five associates we have identified through the Drug Squads network throughout the state. These five have set up drug dealing operations in Gladstone, Rockhampton, Mackay, Townsville and Cairns. Those are all ports where ships ply their trade, making them ideal for smuggling in drugs. They have the whole eastern seaboard sewn up; it appears.'

'Wow, that's some operation,' indicated Sam. 'I have also been talking to Senior Sergeant Mick Jenkins from Karumba police. He was successful in getting a guy named Bernie McInerney to agree to give evidence against my kidnappers, Curly Jacobs and Charlie Briggs, for the guarantee of a lighter prison sentence. Bernie was one of the two whose boat I commandeered to escape from that deserted island. Curly and Charlie were the ones I'd initially approached to supply me with drugs when I was trying to appear to be a drug dealer to get evidence of their illegal operation as cattle rustlers. They were the ones suspected of stealing my uncle's cattle. So, it appears Curly Jacobs and Charlie Briggs could be part of a state-wide operation. Do you think there's a chance they're the kingpins of the entire organisation? The drug importation through the Gulf of Carpentaria was thought to involve the mother ships, which come from all parts of the world for the famous Gulf King Prawns and other tropical fish. So, who knows what they were bringing in?'

'It's turning out to be bigger than originally thought. The Drug Squad, in unison with police in each of the areas along the coast of Queensland, are putting in place a plan to carry out a coordinated raid to net their entire operation in one swoop. That's likely to take place when you're in Townsville.'

'When I give evidence implicating Curly Jacobs and Charlie Briggs in my kidnapping and Bernie McInerney gives his evidence involving them in the supply of drugs to him and his partner, that should guarantee their conviction on those charges. Whatever happens with the state-wide raid will then be additional to our case with extra charges possible, for which they'll be liable to a longer prison sentence. Plus, Bob Scott has them on charges of rustling cattle from cattle properties in Central Queensland and from my uncle's property in the Gulf Savannah. They'll be lucky to see the light of day for a very long time.'

'There's one other thing I have to advise you of. Because of the reference made by Jessie Cameron to him being part of an organisation resembling a snake with multiple heads, we are taking the precaution of getting you a doppelgänger to impersonate you arriving in Townsville. That way, we hope to draw out any potential threat to your safety. He won't be an exact double, but a police office of similar height, build and features to you. As it was reported, you had sustained head injuries when attacked in Brisbane, so he'll have his head partially bandaged and body armour under his suit. If another attacker makes an appearance, we'll have plain-clothes detectives pretending to be reporters and cameramen surrounding him. We're also exploring the possibility that Reece Roberts and your Brisbane attacker Jessie Cameron are both part of the drug syndicate and they have been trying to stop you from giving evidence at the Townsville trial implicating Jacobs and Briggs. It seems they're all part of one gang.'

Letitia had been sitting silently beside Sam while Amos was explaining what was going to happen regarding plans for his safety. Gradually her face mirrored the feeling of relief she was experiencing with the welcome news.

'I can't tell you how happy you have made me feel with your visit,' she signalled. 'There just seems to have been no letup in the ongoing drama and stress ever since the abduction of Ranger Stacey in Carnarvon Gorge. You tire of going around looking over your shoulder all the time for new threats. Your visit, Amos, has made us so relieved. Thank you.'

After Amos had departed, Letitia sank into Sam's arms and broke down in uncontrollable tears. Sam was concerned that her show of emotion was either a signal of her feeling of joy she had just expressed to Amos or something deeper that he was not aware of.

'Are you okay, darling? I thought you'd be smiling rather than crying,' confided Sam.

'Oh Sam, it's like the wall of a dam being breached to at last feel free from the drama of the last few months, but especially the pain I felt when I thought I might lose you in similar circumstances to how Michael was killed. I've been keeping all my sadness and grief bottled up with the possibly of having the same thing happen again. I just couldn't contain the pressure any longer. It has totally burst out. I feel so much lighter now with that burden lifted from my mind.' As she uttered those words, Sam gently wrapped his arms around Letitia and softly kissed her lips as tears continued to flow. Her tears intermingled with his as they embraced.

Letitia took Sam's hand and led him to the bedroom where they lay and made passionate love slowly and with care considering Sam's recovery, in the process wiping away the memory of a chapter in their lives which they were happy to have buried and forgotten. Hopefully for the rest of their lives.

Chapter Twenty-Six

The following ten days leading up to their departure for Townsville were spent in blissful abandon, their love seeming to have multiplied because of the greater appreciation they now had for the life they shared. A life that they treasured more than ever, knowing how easily Sam's life could have been taken away.

The Friday of their departure arrived way too soon, as the demands of Sam appearing in court didn't seem to be of any great relevance except for finally knowing his kidnappers from Karumba wouldn't be able to cause them any more harm.

On their arrival at Townsville airport, Sam and Letitia, along with the police officer acting as Sam's double, were whisked quickly away in separate vehicles and transported to the Grand Chancellor Hotel. News had leaked out, purposely, that the principal witness in the forthcoming trial of accused kidnappers and drug dealers, Curly Jacobs and Charlie Briggs, was arriving in town today. Several press representatives were on hand when Sam's substitute was escorted through the front entrance of the hotel, surrounded by several police officers wearing bullet-proof vests. After their secret escort from the police aircraft, the vehicle carrying Sam and Letitia was driven to a back entrance of the hotel. They alighted from the vehicle and were taken unobserved to their private suite on an upper level.

That evening on the local television, Sam's double, complete with bandaged head, was featured on the news. Likewise, the Townsville Bulletin next morning featured a front-page news item with a photograph of the same person with a bandaged head, supposedly Sam Mackenzie, entering the Grand Chancellor. It expanded on the television story by recounting how Sam had been attacked and suffered a life-threatening brain injury requiring him to be placed in an induced coma. The purpose of the publicity would have the required effect of attracting the attention of another person wanting to stop Sam from giving evidence at the trial on Monday.

When Monday morning dawned and the local press were gathering around the entrance to the Townsville Court House to get publicity shots to feature on lunchtime news broadcasts, the next chapter in the police plan was about to be enacted. Amongst the various news outlets involving journalists from the Townsville Bulletin, interviewers from radio stations and cameramen and reporters from local TV stations, there were also undercover police acting as press representatives. The waiting throng was being observed via CCTV and fed to an enclosed police van parked close by. Their purpose was to pick out anyone in the press gathering who local police could determine was not known to them and, therefore, was suspicious.

Detective Sergeant Amos Billings was one of the undercover press people and through his earpiece, he was being fed minute by minute information. When he received the advice of a cameraman and a reporter who sparked the interest of the chief observer in the van, Amos alerted two of his fellow undercover officers, and they moved towards the suspicious couple. As these two moved within about four metres of where Sam's double was trying to force his way through the throng of press representatives, he saw the pretend reporter with the microphone reach his hand into the inside of his coat and emerge with a knife. Amos and one of the undercover police immediately leapt and tackled the intending assailant to the ground. The other undercover officer took off after the cameraman who had thrown his camera away and was running down Walker Street, turning left on Stokes Street, heading towards Ross Creek. On arriving there, the perp jumped in fully clothed, but the police officer quickly discarded his shirt, pants and boots and dived into the water. He was a strong swimmer quickly reaching the perp who attempted to punch the police officer. He grabbed on firmly to his assailant and pushed his head under the water. He flailed and thrashed about, resulting in him inhaling so much water that on being pulled to the surface he surrendered, a spluttering mess and all out of fight. Both he and Amos's prisoner were transported to police headquarters for intense questioning.

Despite the drama that unfolded prior to the court case about which the local press had obtained a terrific coverage, the trial proceeded on schedule. Sam was called first to give his evidence about his encounter with Curly Jacobs and Charlie Briggs and how they had one of their henchmen assault him before Jacobs and Briggs took him out in their boat to a deserted island in the Gulf of Carpentaria where he was abandoned. Next to be called by the prosecutor was Bernie McInerney, who supplied evidence that he and his accomplice had been supplied drugs from a *mother ship* supposedly in the Gulf to collect seafood for markets in Asia. McInerney confirmed their contact to access the drugs from that ship was Curly Jacobs and his partner, Charlie Briggs. Bernie also recounted the story of how he and his accomplice had landed on the island where Sam Mackanzie had been abandoned, unbeknown to them. They later found out it was Sam who had taken off in their boat with a load of their drugs aboard while they were under the influence of their own drugs and unaware their camp site had been raided by Sam Mackenzie while they were *stoned*.

Senior Sergeant Mick Jenkins from the Karumba police finally sealed the fate of Jacobs and Briggs when he provided evidence of their drug dealings following a surprise and coordinated raid resulting in the arrest of the captain and crew of one of the *mother ships* supplying drugs to them. Both Curly Jacobs and Charlie Briggs were found guilty of being the ringleaders in the drug syndicate operating out of Karumba and also the charges relating to the attack and kidnapping of police officer Sam Mackenzie. The same day as the trial was happening, the coordinated forces of the Queensland Drug Squad carried out raids on drug dealers who were part of the same syndicate. They arrested the chief perpetrators in Cairns, Townsville,

Mackay, Rockhampton and Gladstone. The drug ring was broken and tens of millions of dollars in illegal drugs were seized, as well as hundreds of thousands of dollars in cash, the proceeds of the illegal sale of drugs. With the *heads of the snake*, as referred to by Sam's attacker, Jessie Cameron, now having been decapitated.

Sam and Letitia and the team of police officers had been responsible for the success of the biggest capture of drugs and drug dealers in police history in Queensland and the smashing of their operation they thought was impenetrable. They justifiably celebrated their victory with a party they would remember for many years to come.

Chapter Twenty-Seven

After all that had happened in Sam and Letitia's world in the last couple of months, it was going to take some time for them to wind down, realign themselves with the patterns of everyday living and start to feel normal again. On a previous trip to Townsville, Sam had visited the Reef HQ Great Barrier Reef Aquarium and was impressed with the educational aspects of how the Reef was presented, especially the underwater displays of marine life and colourful presentations of actual growing coral. He vowed and declared that when he had the opportunity again, he would visit the outer Great Barrier Reef to see those features in their natural state. The bonus in this instance was that now he could share the experience with Letitia.

Sam investigated many advertised tours and decided on a Reef Encounter 3-day 2-night Live Aboard tour, departing Cairns. The highlight would be the opportunity to snorkel or do an introduction to diving on the actual Great Barrier Reef, one of the seven natural wonders of the world, acclaimed for its sheer size, which could be seen from outer space. With their Indigenous heritage, they both loved to immerse themselves into the natural world. For Letitia, she was fortunate to live and work in the natural wonder of the inland oasis that was the Carnarvon Gorge National Park, her ancestors' country, the land of the Karingbal people and also the Bidjara and Kara Kara First Nations people.

Sam had been inducted into the great outdoors of the Gulf Savannah region, which his forebears roamed and protected for thousands of years. However, since he left the area to live and work in Queensland's capital city, Brisbane, he'd become immersed by necessity into adopting full-blown big city life and missed the feel of being in his country, the land of the Kalkadoon First Nations people. The Great Barrier Reef was going to be a new and exciting experience for two people whose origin and upbringing revolved around the inland or outback of Australia.

Letitia was surprised and excited with Sam's news of visiting the outer Great Barrier Reef. 'Oh Sam, that's been a dream of mine for so long. To now have the chance to experience it with *the man of my dreams* is beyond believable. When can we go?'

'I've booked a trip departing next Monday, so that gives us several days to take a leisurely drive up the coast to Cairns and enjoy some of the tourist attractions along the way. We can destress as we go, arriving in a state of mind to fully appreciate and enjoy being able to swim and snorkel on one of the great natural wonders of the world.'

The countryside as they drove north gradually changed from the drier tropical climate of Townsville to the greener, more lush vegetation of the wet tropics. The change became more defined after passing through the coastal tropics of Mission Beach and Cardwell, gateway to beautiful offshore islands such as Bedarra, a peaceful tropical getaway to revive flagging spirits. They passed Tully, which had on average the highest rainfall annually of any town in Australia. Rainfall in the area was measured in feet rather than inches. Because of that amount of rain, the road from there to Cairns featured on either side a green wall of sugar cane, with the occasional break where a banana plantation took precedence.

The city of Cairns had a real tropical feel with everything so green, the warmth and humidity contributing factors in it being titled the capital of the Tropics. Sam and Letitia had a couple of leisurely days acquainting themselves with tourist sites and attractions like the historical train trip to Kuranda, through areas of lush tropical rainforest. On their return journey, they were enthralled with the Skyrail Rainforest Cableway, which afforded them a spectacular aerial ride above the treetop canopy with two stops to enjoy a visit to the CSIRO Interpretive centre or a rainforest walk.

When the Cableway arrived at Smithfield, another highlight for them, being of Indigenous heritage themselves, was a visit to the Tjapukai Aboriginal Cultural Centre and to experience the Night Fire by Aboriginal Tjapukai Show. They learned about the local legends of the Dreamtime and discovered, through traditional dances, music and storytelling, the way of life for the Indigenous people of the tropics. Monday soon came around and they boarded early, the catamaran taking them to the Reef Encounter. The floating resort was surrounded by crystal clear waters in the middle of the Great Barrier Reef, where for the next few days they could experience the magic of the natural wonder. First, they had to learn to snorkel, although they were both excellent swimmers. The key skill was to learn the breathing technique so that in diving beneath the surface, you remembered to hold your breath. A few mouthfuls of salt water soon taught one how to do it correctly.

Sam and Letitia spent as much time as possible during daylight hours snorkelling down to the columns of the coral reefs. They found the soft corals displayed the most vibrant colours, with their bright pinks and mauves. These were the homes of marine species such as tropical fish of many colours and shapes, prawns, sea slugs, and occasionally swimming majestically by a greenback turtle. All their diving built up an appetite with their hunger catered for by a sumptuous smorgasbord of tropical salads, seafoods and tropical fruits. Each night the tropical atmosphere lent itself to mixing with a variety of guests from many parts of the world and enjoying the stories of their travels. That interested Sam and Letitia, as overseas travel was something they hoped to do in the future. Their double bed was a welcome sight after an action filled day of exploration as they embraced and made beautiful love with the gentle rocking of the marine vessel seeming to accompany the movement of their bodies until they reached the heights of extreme physical passion.

As they lay in the afterglow of their complete abandonment to being in the present moment, Sam and Letitia felt more alive than at any time since they'd met some six months prior. Sam was particularly imbued with the emotion of what it all meant, having also experienced in that time the uncertainty of life from the physically violent attacks upon him by criminal elements.

'You know, Letitia, this world can be a place of much hatred, violence and greed, but what balances it all out is that our love is the personification of who we are and where we come from, our ancestors, our traditions, our country. They are a part of us and we are a part of them. We are a part of all that surrounds us, a part of nature. We are in nature and nature is a part of us, combined as one. Just like us, united by the most powerful force in nature: love. Out here on the waters of the Great Barrier Reef I can't think of a more appropriate time than to ask you, beautiful lady and my hope for the future, *will you make me the happiest man alive and agree to marry me?*'

Letitia was overwhelmed as the proposal was unexpected, even though her thoughts had focused on the possibility in recent times. With tears appearing in her eyes and a smile lighting up her face, she embraced Sam, kissing his lips passionately. *'Yes, my beautiful darling man. Yes...Yes...Yes. A thousand times, Yes. Nothing would give me greater joy than to be your wife and loving you all the days of our lives.'*

As their bodies moulded together once more and their spirits soared in ecstasy to the heavens, they felt totally complete, moving in unison from the magic of making *love under the Milky Way*, with its brightness personified by the clarity of the sky out on the ocean, combining with the beauty of the moon, beaming through their cabin window clothing their nakedness in a silvery veil of light, revealing in its brilliance the promise of a new creation. They were immersed in their own universe with love as the centre, like a life-giving sun.

It was almost twelve months since Chloe, Sam's first true love, was taken from him tragically. *'How could I be so fortunate,'* he reasoned, *'to be loved by two of the most kind, intelligent, passionate, beautiful and understanding women*?'

'I am indeed a lucky man,' he acknowledged, as he physically embraced Letitia, while mentally recalling the warmth and caring nature of Chloe. 'You will always hold *a place in my heart,'* he silently promised her, 'as will our son Waru, who I wish I could have met. True love lives on forever, so this is not goodbye, but as the Germans say, *auf Wiedersehen, until we meet again*. Even though I love Letitia now, how could I ever forget you, Chloe? You taught me the meaning of Love.'

CPSIA information can be obtained
at www.ICGtesting.com
Printed in the USA
LVHW040621201222
735554LV00012B/640

9 780645 391640